Maddox

Ravenwood Academy Book Three

Maddox

Copyright © 2024 by C L Easton

Cover Design: Black Pirate Book Cover

Publisher: Black Rose Publishing

Ebook ISBN: 978-1-998910-12-0

Paperback ISBN: 978-1-998910-13-7

Maddox

Ravenwood Academy Book Three

C. L. EASTON

"I dread the events of the future,
not in themselves but in their
results."
-Edgar Allan Poe

Author Note

Welcome back to Ravenwood Academy For the Last Time.

The last book in the series. Are you ready to say goodbye?

Dub-Con/Non-Con, Alcohol and Drug Abuse, Mention of S.A, Rehab, Rough Sex, Detailed Sex Scenes, Torture, Talk of Parental Death.

Playlist

Pure Morning- Placebo
I'd Rather Overdose- honestav, Z
All I Wanted- Paramore
Bite Marks- Ari Abdul
I Remember Everything- Zach Bryan,
Kacey Musgraves
Pumpin Blood- NONONO
Come a Little Closer- Cage The Elephant
Out of My League- Fitz and The Tantrums
Team- Lorde
I'm So Sick- Flyleaf

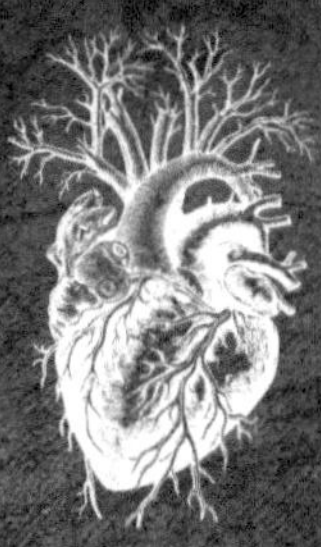

Playlist

You're Going Down- SICK PUPPIES
Float On- Modest Mous
It's Alright- Mother Mother
Habits(Steay High) Hippie Sabotage
Remix- Tove. Love
It's Called: Freefall- Rainbow Kitten
Surprise
Angel- Massive Attack. Horace Andy

One

Jinx

I don't want to be around anyone. Clicking the door to my dorm felt like a relief if only it could stay that way. Weeks have gone by, but the thoughts have never left me. I thought I was strong enough to get around every day. However, that was a joke.

The school halls remind me of Dad, and I haven't stepped foot inside his office since the last time. I told Florence she was on her own with the new dean. Regarding the new dean, Allan has been brought on board, and I strongly encouraged him to consider hiring a new music professor.

Von needs to go. I'm tired of his shit. It's time to clean up this school if only a new board member cleanup were allowed. That would also be on the list.

A pointed tap on my window pulls a smile to my face, Edgar. I push the window open and wait for him to hop in. With a shake of his head and, I swear, a pissed-off look, he jumps onto the counter.

"Kraa."

"Yeah, I got it." Still no patience. At this point, I'm pretty sure the fucker will never get any. I open his treat jar, and he does a little dance to where I'm standing. After digging out a few treats and laying them out for him, I watch as he snatches them, eating them whole.

"Don't be such a pig."

He cranks his head in my direction and makes his little bubba sounds. The glare he gives me, if he weren't such a cute bird, I would throw him out. It's peaceful having the dorm to myself. I asked the boys to drop me off so that I could have some alone time with my cello. I'm feeling a bit disappointed that I didn't get that spot in the symphony again. I just need some space to process it all.

I clean my dorm while Edgar naps his treats off. I'm trying to keep my mind off things, wondering when this fog will lift so I can return to normal. When I think everything is under control, I stumble upon something of Dad's, and my world crashes again. The last time that I went to the house was before the funeral. I don't have it in me to go through his things. It also doesn't help that Serena still calls every other day.

Today was the will reading; as I had imagined, that didn't go well. It's another reason why I need to be left alone. Serena sucks the energy right out of a person. She should've believed me in the first place, and that she would have walked away with nothing. Marrying a person because they are well off isn't a good reason. I'm glad Dad saw that because Serena is a snake, and even now, she's trying her hardest to take what isn't hers. I'll never give her a cent; she'll have to kill me first.

"Kraa."

"Sorry, mister." I turn to Edgar, who is now awake and is tapping on the window to be let back outside. "Give me a minute. That patience we've been talking about. You need to work on them." I head back to the counter to open the window. Just as I'm about to push it open, Edgar suddenly raises his head and looks towards the door. I turn to see what caught his attention but don't hear anything.

"Get your ass outside. Come back when you feel the need to harass me again." I push the window open for him, but he doesn't move. He continues to stare at the door.

"Only because I love you. I'll check the door." My heart knocks against my chest when I take a step forward. If it's true about what they say about animals, I hope he sensed nothing. With slow, light steps, I make it to the door, unlocking it as quietly as possible. I take one last deep inhale and swing it open.

Nothing, no one is there.

"Edgar, you fucker. You scared me for no reason." As I start to close the door, something catches my eye. A bundle of sheet music and a single black rose lay in front of my door. I peek around the doorframe, but the hall is empty. Maybe one of the guys dropped it off for me?

It's nice that they are listening to me and giving me the space I desperately need. I toss the sheet music on the coffee table, move to the sink, and find a glass. I'm not one to keep vases around; I hardly ever receive flowers. Placing the single rose in the water, I admire it. It's nice to get flowers occasionally, even if they eventually die. It serves as a gentle reminder that lovely moments are fleeting, urging you to treasure them while you can. They have a way of slipping away effortlessly, slipping through your grasp.

Edgar flies over and lands next to the flower. It's a small reminder that one day, I'll lose him too. We both stare at the flower for a short time. When I look at Edgar, he's already staring at me.

"What are you thinking about, my feathered friend?" He cocks his head to the side, blinking. "Yeah, that's what I thought. The window is open, and you can get on with your day. Thank you for the visit."

Once he hops back to the window, he doesn't waste any time flying away; he lets out his kraa when he reaches the trees and disappears. I hope one day Edgar finds a mate. He can't always be coming around, no matter how much I enjoy it. He'll be lonely one day.

I watch the tree blow. No matter how often I stare into the woods, it never settles in my stomach. Something hides in there, and maybe it's the same thing that hides in the school's basement—Evil. When I finally can't handle it any longer, I turn away. The sheet music grabs my attention, picking it up. I wonder what kind it is. I've never let anyone pick my music unless it was a professor. I'm rather picky.

It's all music I wouldn't pick for myself, and I wouldn't have pictured one of the guys picking either. Playing covers isn't usually my thing, and I've only done it for Maddox once. Maybe he dropped this off.

Me: Thanks for the Sheet music and flower

Maddox: I don't know what you're talking about, baby. Maybe one of the twins?

Me: Maybe

Well, I thought it was him for sure.

Me: Did you drop a little gift off at my door?

Ashton: Wasn't me, Little Swan. What was it?

Me: Sheet music and a black rose

Ashton: Maddox? It sounds like something he would do.

Me: He said it wasn't him. I'll try Atticus.

If it were Atticus, I'd be shocked. He doesn't seem like a gift-giving kind of person.

Me: Are you a romantic gift-giver?

Atticus: No, Little Grim. Don't ever expect a romantic gesture from me. Why?

It couldn't be Spencer. We never do this sort of thing.

Me: A gift was left at my door, and it wasn't any of you guys. Now I'm starting to freak out.

Atticus: What kind of gift, Jinx?

Me: A black rose and sheet music

Only one other person comes to mind, but if it were him, he would've sent me a text bragging about his little gift. *Unknown* loves to prove that he never misses a chance to make my life a living hell, even if I'm already there. He won't tell me why he chose me even after all these months—three months, and there is still no hint of why he stalks me. I can't even think of why, and it bugs me daily.

I flip through all the sheet music, looking for a clue as to who would've dropped this off, but nothing has come up so far. There has to be over ten pieces alone. Why would they give me so much? A single piece of white paper tucked in between catches my eye.

I carefully remove and unfold it. The words written in red ink almost jump off the page at me.

> *A single black rose to take a life*
> *A single black rose to make you cry*

A single black rose to make you think

What in the fuck. Who would give me this? And why? Is that what the rose means? Oh my God, there are so many questions running through my head I can't keep track of them. Whoever sent it never bothered to sign it. Why send it if you don't want me to know who you are? What a coward. I don't know what any of this means, and I don't have the brainpower to think anymore.

I gather all the paper. There's no way I'm keeping this music around if it has a hidden message within; walking to the garbage, I toss it all in. Turning to the rose, shivers roll down my back. Roses are supposed to be romantic, not morbid, not a reminder that I have lost a loved one.

I quickly snatch the rose from the vase and dump it in the trash. I don't need a reminder of the gift. I can't get the words from that note out of my head. What if the killer left this?

Me: Are you in your dorm?

Pencil: No, but you can hang if you need to, I'm almost finished with class. What's wrong?

Me: Nothing. Don't worry. I'll be in there when you get done.

Pencil: Teeny, don't lie to me.

I hate that he knows me so well. I can't hide anything from him, even in text.

Me: I'll explain when you get there.

I toss my phone on the couch and head into my bedroom. I need to change into something comfy if it's going to be a best friend kind of night. We haven't had one of those in months, and sometimes, you need a good get together with the bestie. And lord knows I need a good catch-up.

I grab a black sweater and a pair of leggings from my closet. Don't get me wrong, I love wearing dresses and skirts, but leggings are the ultimate comfort and one piece of clothing I'll never give up, that and knee-high socks. I open the top dresser drawer and stare at all my socks. Does one person honestly need this many pairs? I grab the first pair, a black and white striped knee-high length. Spence always keeps his place on the colder side, so this works out perfectly.

Poking my head out into the hall, making sure it's clear I leave my dorm. That gift has made me paranoid now. What if that person is still hanging around? I quickly jog down the stairs, getting to Spence's place in no time. I open his door, and I'm met with a disaster. I should've known better that it wouldn't be clean; he needs to get out of this place more. A trip to the city would do it. But I haven't been in the mood for that, and it's unfair to him.

While I wait, I get busy cleaning. It's the least I can do, considering I'm about to drop some news on Spence. This way, all throwable objects are cleaned up. I haven't updated him on the stalker in a while, but now a mysterious gift has arrived. He'll have his theories, but they won't be good. And that's what scares me the most.

Spencer isn't scared to speak his mind, either.

Two

Jinx

I'm pouring myself a drink when the door swings open, and a distressed Spencer stumbles in. His gray eyes scan the room until they land on me. His shoulders relax as he steps further inside once he sees everything is fine.

"Teeny, you had me stressing hardcore. I couldn't even focus on the chick in front of me in the last class. That's how much you fucked me up."

"Spence, she'll be there tomorrow, like every day. Don't be a pussy and ask her out already."

He places a hand over his heart and raises his brow in shock. "No, I can't do that. I need to fantasize about our life." He walks over to me and grabs the vodka.

"And how is that goin'?" I sip on my cranberry and vodka while Spence makes his drink.

"I've made progress in my fantasy, but I have a feeling she won't live up to my dreams." He shrugs. "It is what it is. I'll be a lone wolf for a while."

I wait for him to sit and drink. I know the question is on the tip of his tongue, and I'm not going to turn into little Miss Debbie downer and shift this conversation into WWIII. He watches me over his glass, knowing I won't speak first.

"Jinx, spill it."

"Spence, it's been a hard day. One more drink, please."

He sets his glass on the counter, walks over to me, and takes my drink without saying a word. He's going to make it a strong one; I know it. He never learned how to pour a decent drink in his life. This drink will make my lips loose, and he'll get answers quickly.

"Chug it. I'm growing impatient here." Spence hands me my glass back, and it's not my cranberry drink.

"What is it?"

"Something stronger, trust me, you'll like it more." The ice clashes against the glass, but the dark liquor worries me.

"No offense, Spencer. But the last time you did this to me, I was in the bathroom, hugging the toilet."

He rolls his eyes. "It's whiskey. Shut up and drink it. Before I make you."

I snatch it from his hands with a growl and slam it back. It's more whiskey than soda. And fuck does it burn going down. Coughing, I hand the glass back to Spence.

"Don't make me another. I'm done."

He pats me on the back. "I'm proud of you, champ. I literally only added enough Coke for color."

"I know." I looked at him with a straight face.

He puckers his lips in a kiss. "Love you too."

I make my way over to the couch and plop down, feeling the weight of the world on my shoulders. How did things end up like this? I guess I'm truly living up to my nickname. I've become a total jinx—everything I touch seems to crumble around me.

"We had the will reading today."

"Fuck. Serena?" He sits beside me, looking directly at me.

I shift to look at him, grabbing the throw blanket covering myself. "Yeah, it was a nightmare, Spence. She wouldn't shut up the entire time. If I made it through this without hearing her voice again, I would be the happiest person on the planet."

"I take it she didn't believe you that she was walking away with dickshit."

"If she did, it would've been easier on the lawyer and me. She wants to take me to court and fight for the house and the school." Just thinking about it turns my stomach.

I can't fight her. There isn't any way to win. What would I do if she did go through with it? I'm fucked.

He pulls my arm and drags me across the couch, getting all up in my face. "That cunt can try to fight, but she won't win. You have an army behind you. Nothing will happen when you have me in your corner. Now tell me what else happened."

I drop my head on his chest. "Spencer, I don't wanna be here anymore."

"As in here or life, Teeny?"

"Depends on the day, if we are being honest." His hand runs through my hair, but it does nothing to calm my racing heart. "Spence, there's something else."

His hand freezes, pulling me closer. "I swear to God, Jinx. I'm going to have to move you in, aren't I?"

"You might. A gift was delivered to my doorstep today." My entire body tenses as I say the words. The thought of the note makes me sick.

"How bad was the gift, Odette?" There was a deep note to his voice.

"I thought it was from one of the guys because it initially seemed sweet. Then, it turned into misery. I think the person responsible for killing my father left it for me."

My surroundings blur as I'm pushed backward. "What the fuck, Jinx. And you just casually tell me this." Spencer stares at me with huge eyes. His nails dig into my arms. "Where is the note?"

"In the garbage. I wasn't keeping anything they gave me."

"And you are sure one of the guys didn't do it, and it's not some kind of sick joke?"

I hall off and punch Spencer in the stomach. "Yes, you asshole. They wouldn't do that."

He coughs, rubbing his stomach. "Fine. I just wanted to make sure, or I would have to hurt them."

"Spencer, I love you and all. But you can't even hurt a fly."

"Just because I don't protect myself doesn't mean I wouldn't protect you, Jinx. I would do anything for you."

His gray gaze is so intense that I need to look away. I've never seen Spence look at me like that before. To be honest, it's freaking me out. He's my best friend, and I know he would go to the end of the earth for me, but I would never ask him to.

"Spence, I love you. But there won't be a need for your mad fighting skills."

He gave a deep sigh, like I had taken away his fun. "Fine. Be that way. Fun sucker." His bottom lip pops out, and he crosses his arms.

"Don't pout." I tug his lip.

He slaps my hand away and gets up. "Are you hungry? We need to move on, or I'm going to do things that I shouldn't."

"Are you cooking, or should I?"

He stops at the edge of his kitchen. "Maybe you should. I am a bachelor, after all, and I cook questionable food."

Oh, that I know. I'll never eat anything Spencer cooks again. My stomach isn't made of steel. The last meal was—interesting. Pasta mixed with peanut butter is one meal I never want to eat again. I feel sorry if he ever gets a girlfriend; she'll be cooking a lot.

"Won't the guys worry that you aren't in your dorm?"

"No. I told them I needed some time alone."

He cocks an eyebrow. "Alone time."

"Not that kind. They get a little clingy sometimes, and I need some breathing space. They'll blow my phone up if they can't find me." I open a cupboard and find nothing but snack food. "Spence, what the fuck have you been eating?"

"Uh, nothing. I've been busy."

I turn slowly, taking in my bestie, the one who will drop everything for a meal. "Busy? Doing what?"

He glances toward the ceiling, avoiding me.

"Spencer Aaron Coldwell, tell me right now."

He clasps his hands around his head, releasing another deep sigh. "I might have started seeing someone." He drops his head, drawing a small smile.

A shit eating grin spreads across my face. "A girl?"

"Yes, a girl, Jesus Jinx." He pushes past me, grabbing a bag of chips. "You might know her."

My stomach drops. If it's Lula, I'll kick him in the nuts.

"Who, Spencer?" My voice shakes.

"Big titties." He grins.

Big titties? Why does that ring a bel- "Spencer! You can't call her that."

"I don't, not to her face or anything. But you bet your ass I say it to the titties." He wiggles his brows.

I shake my head. "Don't need to know what goes on between you and River."

"It's nothing serious, just some fun time. Since I won't be sticking around this town after school."

"How do you know she doesn't want anything serious?" I steal a few of his chips.

He chuckles. "Trust me, if River is sleeping with me, she doesn't want anything serious." He pushes his glasses up his nose.

"Spencer. You're a great guy, don't say shit like that. If she can't see who you truly are, she doesn't deserve to have you in her life, period. You need someone who enjoys the same things you do and wants to celebrate life's joys. Not because you can get her off in bed. Jesus, her fingers can do that. Don't you ever stoop low, do you understand?"

He squeezes the bag of chips. "Do the guys make you feel that way?" he asked with a touch of disapproval.

Maddox supports me musically. We both love playing together. I know he also wanted to get into the orchestra, even if he didn't tell me. But he never treated anything like a competition; we're a team. And we still are.

Ashton is calming. He's there to pull me out even when I'm drowning in myself. That's one thing about Ashton: he'll never let you go too far. He knows when you need help; until then, he never steps over that line.

Atticus. He infuriates me like there is no tomorrow. It's like his life mission to piss me off, but deep down, it's because he cares. Then again, it also makes me wonder if he only does it because he still hates me. It's the small details that run through my mind, the switch of the phone. How else would *Unknown* have known that it was switched? Even after telling me to be safe in public, Atticus has no problem having sex out in the open. Is it possible that he and Roan were involved in this the entire time?

"Jinx? What's wrong?"

I stumble to the couch, placing my head in my hands. "I'm not feeling so good, Spence. I think I've been getting lied to this entire time."

"What? From who?" He kneels in front of me, taking my chin in his hand.

"Atticus, I think he knows my stalker."

A vein ticked along his temple as anger discolored his face. "I'm gonna kill that motherfucker. Where the fuck is he." He storms to the door, grabbing a baseball bat.

I bolt upright. "Spencer, stop. I don't have proof."

"I'll show you proof, his fucking blood on the ground. Change your lock code, don't let that cunt in your dorm, don't you be alone with him. He lost my fucking trust, Odette." His eyes spewed fire.

I cross the room and slowly grab the baseball bat from Spencer's hand. "Let me get some evidence first, and then I promise you can get your blood. But until then, remain civil."

His face screwed into a scowl. "You have a week. Start digging."

A week. That's not enough time. How the hell can I find anything on him? It's not like I can go around and ask his brother or Maddox. It looks like it'll be another stakeout mission, this time with one of my boyfriends.

Three

Maddox

There has been something different about RWA ever since Prescott passed away. It's like this place isn't safe anymore, but I can't explain why; I feel it in my bones. Since yesterday, Jinx has been avoiding us. She even went as far as changing her door code, permanently locking us out.

I don't know what I did wrong. My mind needs answers, but I can only give it a bottle of Jack. But one bottle turns into two, and that's when I finally feel numb, and nothing matters, sadly not even Jinx. I want to find an end to her stalker problem, but what can I do? I'm a fuckin' loser.

I'm torturing myself again by driving back into Grovedale. It's like I have unfinished business with this moronic town. The pull is still strong, and I need to cut the cord; the only way to do that is to talk to her. My chest tightens the closer the town limits are, and I don't think I can do this without a drop of liquor in my system. But I know if I drink, shit won't go my way. She has a way of manipulating me if she smells booze on my breath.

The house is nothing but a shell from when I burnt it down, a reminder that nothing is meant to last forever and, in the end, only your bones will be left behind. Soon, you'll be nothing, not even a memory, and people will go back to their lives like it was nothing.

Hell, some don't even wait for you to be dead to forget about you.

I keep driving to the motel she always stays at; she's like a creature of habit, nothing ever changes. The Blackbird Motel might have been the best in its prime now. It's barely standing. All the doors are faded gray and the bricks are practically falling off the walls. Honestly, this place really needs to be bulldozed into the ground.

I pull up in front of room 6. This room haunts my dreams to this day. The terror didn't stay in that house. I would burn this place down if that were possible, and then maybe I would sleep peacefully for once. The thought of my past being swept away almost brings me joy.

The steering wheel bites into my skin the harsher I squeeze. Whatever happens behind that door, I won't soon forget, and I only hope she's alone. With a final heavy exhale and a push to the door, I exit the car, leaving my sanctuary and replacing it with purgatory. I can't do this for much longer. I need to cut ties.

The boardwalk leading to each room is broken and uneven, another reason for this building to be torn down. Standing in front of room 6, my heart is trying to jump out of my chest. Raising my hand to knock, the door flings open, and I come face to face with the woman I want to forget.

"Well, if it isn't the worthless son." Smoke slid from her dainty nose.

I stare down at her, taking all of her in. Messy, limp chocolate brown hair that probably hasn't seen a shower or a hairbrush in weeks. She had a smoke dangling from her lips and another one glowing between her slightly stained fingers. Her dull skin doesn't see much sun from the looks of it, and I wonder if she's eaten anything in the last—fuck, why do I care. Her stained band tee is all I need to know about her living conditions, and remember, she never gave a fuck about me when I was growing up.

"From where I'm standing, I'm not the worthless one, Mom."

She flicks her smoke at me, and sparks fly as they bounce off my chest. "Watch your mouth. Do you think you're better than me just because you are in a fancy school? Think again, Maddox. You'll always be a worthless piece of shit. No one cares about you, and if they say they do, they are lying to you. How could anyone love a nobody like you."

Her words cut me until I'm bleeding at her feet. She doesn't even have to lay a hand on me anymore. She lets the words take over. No matter how much I want to ignore them, they sink deep, biting to the bone. I try not to show the pain, but the smirk spreading across her face tells me she knows.

"Got nothin' to say?" she asks with a smoke hanging from her cracked lips.

I swallow the lump and ask the question I've been wondering about my entire life. "Why do you hate me so much?" Sweat beads down my back when her eyes narrow, and I'm grateful that smoke isn't lit.

She pulled the smoke from her lips, pinching it between her fingers. Taking a step toward me, her bony finger drives into my chest. "I despise you, Maddox. You ruined my entire life." Her face lights up with anger. "I could've been someone, but you came along and blew all my dreams out of the water. Why couldn't you perish when I gave you all those pills."

Nausea grips my stomach muscles. I stare down at her finger, wondering how she could touch me even after all these years. Wrapping my hand around her wrist, I push her back, watching her tumble to the floor.

"If I disgust you so fuckin' much, why do you still torture me so much? Why can't you leave me alone for once in your pathetic life?" Rage shot through me as I screamed at her.

Her laughter was low and throaty. "I'm not the one that keeps returning now, am I?" She defiantly lifts her chin and smiles thinly. "What do you want, Maddox?"

Having Dad yell my name only meant one thing. It was time to head out of the house for what he would call a life mission. I'm not sure what I was meant to be learning. I can hardly tie my shoes. I hate leaving the house with him. He's mean.

"Let's go, you little rodent. We have shit to do."

I'm barely off the last step, and he snatches my arm, making me trip over my feet. Before I hit the floor, he lifts me in the air. Pain shoots down my arm into my shoulder. I know better than to cry out, which would lead to a smack across the face.

"I don't understand why I need to go?" I asked once he placed me down.

The smack was hard and quick, and it left my cheek sting- ing. But I still knew better than to scream in pain. I slowly walked to the front door, not looking back.

The life mission that I need to learn today is how to break into cars. I learned a lot of things that day, especially how to outrun the cops when you try to break into the mayor's son's car. No one said my dad was smart.

Of course, he blamed me because I picked the car. How was I supposed to know? The car looked cool. Mom gave me ice cream with white chocolate chips that night, but they tasted bitter.

That was the night she tried to kill me because I almost got her husband arrested for fucking up a job. How, as a six-year-old, supposed to know better? They should've handed me over to the state if they didn't want me. Anything would've been better.

"I guess I need closure. I want to walk away and forget that you exist. If you want me dead so bad, maybe it'll happen. But I swear to God, if you or Dad ever come back into my life, I won't think twice about burning you down with me." Before I lose it further or she can say anything, I turn and walk away.

My heart pounds until I'm seated behind the safety of my steering wheel. The engine's roar almost calms me, but I need something else. I peel out of the parking lot, spitting gravel behind me. I need to add distance between her fast. That night didn't feel real, and the ice cream should've been a tip-off. Desserts never happened in that hell. But I was excited to be getting something sweet, and by my mom, at the time, I didn't think twice about shoveling the entire bowl down my throat. I'm not sure how I survived, but they have acted even colder toward me since then. I belong to only one place, even if I don't want to be there.

When I pull into the RWA gate, I regret coming back here. It's the same cycle. Should I stay or go? It's been weighing on my mind for weeks, and I'm unsure what to do. And the same reason to stay keeps me here. Jinx.

But is that enough? It needs to be, or what else is there? I'm pissed with Von. He announced the winners of the symphony, and surprise, surprise, it was Lula. Jinx was right about everything; he'll make the person he's sleeping with the winner. He needs to be stopped.

Since I'm still full of rage, I plan to bring Von down for good. Not that anything I've ever planned before worked out, but here's to hoping. I swing into the staff parking and find Von's car. The douche thinks he's a hotshot and drives a Mustang. Not even an older one. It's one from the '90s.

The only thing I'm thankful for is Dad teaching me how to break into vehicles. I park next to the hot red Mustang, leaving my Impala running; this won't take long. I grab a bag from the trunk with an arson of tools. I move to the driver's side of the Mustang. Digging into my bag, I grab the slim jim and shimmy it into the door. Before I blink, the lock pops—years of practice.

I quickly pop the hood, and moving to the front of the car, I pull the power steering wire and wiggle the battery loose. Then I move to the driver's side, slicing a small cut into his break line. Von won't be getting far. I'll be patiently waiting for him. This might be better than drinking; the thought of waiting for my prey sends my body into overdrive. After I relock his door, I hop back into my car, reverse into the far parking spot, and wait. Von never stays on school grounds late. I'm nailing him hard once he realizes he can't drive that far.

The slam of a car door jerks me awake. Von is in his gray pin-striped pants and a wrinkled navy dress shirt. His graying hair is a mess, which tells me he had a go around with Lula. I guess if she wants to keep that spot, she had better keep him satisfied. His car hesitates to start, and I can't help but laugh.

Oh, this is going to be too easy.

I pull out a few seconds after he does, making sure to stay a couple of feet behind. It won't take long until he realizes his brakes are failing. I'm sure he's already noticed his steering is stiff enough to turn. We're coming up to the first stop sign, and my heart jumps when his brake lights flash for a split second—his car veers off the road, heading for the ditch. Von's car slams into the ditch, which is very anticlimactic. I hoped it would've rolled a few times, maybe burst into flames. One could dream.

Instead, all I hear when I step out of my car is the sound of the horn blaring. Ten buck says the cunt knocked himself out cold. Taking my time, I trudge over and pry open the driver's door.

The sight before me does indeed make me smile. Von is passed the fuck out, and blood slowly drips from a gash just above his eye. Unfortunately, it's not a wound that will kill him; he'll wake up with a bad headache.

I bow downward, ducking inside his car. The smell of blood coated the air with a metallic taste. I grip the back of his seat and lean next to his ear. "I know you can hear me, asshole. Let this be a lesson. Don't fuck with a Van Daren. Because the next time, you won't be breathing." I resist the urge to slam his face into the steering wheel, so I turn and walk away.

This seems to be my motto for the day—walking away.

Four

Ashton

Being friends with Maddox has always been a blessing. But lately, he's been on a downward spiral, and I'm unsure how to help him. I can't keep holding his hand when shit goes south. He needs to figure some shit out for himself, and I know with Jinx blocking herself from him again doesn't help. But he can't always count on other people, either.

And by the state of his body lying on the bathroom floor tells me everything I need to know. Another bender, and he breathes an additional day. I'm not sure how much I have left in me to keep picking him up day after day. I'm afraid one day will be the last.

Gently rolling him onto his back, I tap his cheek. "Hey, Mad. Rise and shine, beauty queen. The birds are singing, so it's time to wake up."

He babbles something, his eyes never twitching.

"Seriously, Maddox. Wake the fuck up," I snap, losing what patience I had. I haul him up by his arm into a seating position. His head falls forward like a broken limb, and his face crumples with pain.

"Ash?" he asked with a rough sigh.

"Yeah, man, it's me."

He cranked his neck, locking our eyes. "I went and saw her. I shouldn't have."

I'm confused by who she is. I know a lot of women, and so does Maddox; he isn't leaving me much to go on. I know it wasn't Jinx. A visit from Jinx wouldn't have caused a downfall. There is no way in hell he would've visited my mom.

"You went and saw your mom? Why, Maddox?" I don't want to sound disappointed, but you can hear it. That woman is nasty.

"I'm a sucker for pain, I suppose. I know it was stupid; save the lecture." He swings his arm, looking for the counter.

I grab his arm, helping him up. "I won't lecture you, but Mad, that woman isn't healthy for you. I thought we talked about this. She can't be in your life anymore. Every time you see her, you end up like this. She plants seeds of doubt, and you allow the roots to take hold, embedding you deep. Only you hold the power to cut them off."

His shoulders slump, losing what fight he had. "She tried to kill me when I was a kid, Ash. That shit is embedded for life. No wonder why I'm such a fuck up. I couldn't even die then."

That fucking bitch, a sense of dread rolls through the pit of my stomach. I can't leave Maddox alone, but I can't let her get away with this, either. Fortunately for her, my priorities are Maddox. Her time will come; she doesn't deserve to breathe the same air as him. He needs to be set free from that life.

"Come on, big guy, let's get you into bed. You need to sleep off some of this booze. You smell worse than the brewery."

"I feel like shit." Shuffling slowly into his room, he ungracefully falls onto the bed. "Leave me." He points his finger into the air.

Maddox is carefree only when he's almost sober; a spark of joy runs through his body, and the child emerges. My heart breaks for him. At least Atticus and I had a decent childhood, but it wasn't until years later that mine crumbled. With the help of Maddox, I made it through, but now I need to help him. Once I hear his snores, I close the door.

When I step back into his kitchen, I finally look around. Garbage lines the small countertop, liquor bottles fill the sink, and there is absolutely no food in this place. I get busy cleaning. It's one thing that'll help keep things off my mind and make me not leave this place and go hunting the fucking bitch down.

That reminds me of my pest problem. Mommy Dearest.

She called after the will reading, complaining that she got nothing. It's not like she didn't have notice, Jinx told her. I wish Ace and I could've been there, but since we were only the stepsons, we weren't allowed inside the lawyer's office. It took me hours to calm her down, and she kept saying the stupidest shit. Mom, can't sue Jinx for the school; it belongs to a board and Jinx. She'll never succeed. It's all a scare tactic to see if Jinx will cave. It won't work.

My next goal is to get Jinx talking again; we have the cold shoulder again for some reason. Her mood swings are getting out of hand. I'm trying to be understanding with the passing of her dad and all, but like fuck. Why are we all getting punished all of a sudden? It came out of nowhere.

I toss the liquor bottles hard into the trash can when I think about it. Leave it to my mom to go after something she can't have. That woman drives me up the fuckin' wall. I'm halfway through cleaning when my phone rings. I take a deep inhale, praying it isn't the witch calling.

"Ace, what's up?" Thank fuck it's him.

"Where the fuck are you? I've been looking every-where."

I snorted a laugh. "You didn't look very good. Use those woman eyes, Atticus. I'm over at Maddox's place."

I can hear a door close and heavy footsteps.

"Are you running?" I ask.

"What the fuck does it sound like, a gentle breeze in the park?" The line goes dead.

I hate when he does that, tucking my phone back into my pocket, and the door opens. Looking at my brother is almost like looking in a mirror sometimes, but this douche had to go out and cover himself in tattoos. I don't blame him—our entire lives; we have been battling for our own identity.

"Where's Maddox?" He asks, closing the door behind him. The further he walks into the small space, the more energy I can feel him suck up. He's pissed about some-thing.

"Sleeping. Why?"

"Has he talked to you?"

I watch him pace around the dorm. His blue eyes flash dangerously when they turn to the bedroom.

"Ace, talk to me. What the fuck is going on?"

He turns back to me. "You know what that asshole did?"

I shrug. It's the reason I asked dickhead. He glares because he knows exactly what I thought.

He points to the room. "That asshole almost killed a professor."

My brows snapped together. "Oh, come on. How the fuck would you know?" I move in front of him, wanting to kick the shit out of him for saying such crap.

"Little does our offender know, the staff parking lot has security cameras. They caught everything, Ash. The worst part is we don't have Prescott here to bail him out. The evidence is clear as day."

"Shit," I spoke lowly. "So what now?"

Atticus leans forward, pressing his palms on his thighs. Staring at the ground, he says, "I'm not sure, but it won't end well for him. You think Von is going to let this slide."

I push a hand through my hair, and every scenario runs through my head. We can't do a fuckin' thing, I'm not even sure Jinx can pull any strings if the cops are involved. Maddox dug himself a hole that even he can't get out of.

"Have you told Jinx?"

"She won't talk to me."

This time, I kick his shin. "What the hell did you do?"

He glares at me, rubbing his leg. "Ouch, you prick. I didn't do shit."

"I'm not fighting, but you must've done something. You're the asshole, anyway."

Atticus always fucks something up, so this doesn't surprise me. He can't keep a cool head even if you pay him. Don't get me wrong, I love the guy, but fuck. How often do we have to go through this before this entire relationship ends? I'm almost at my melting point. The ups are amazing, but I can't handle the downs, and I'm nearly ready to walk away from them.

Being in the dorm is suffocating me, and it's only going to piss me off if I don't leave soon. If I don't distract myself quickly, I'm going to blow my top. Without saying a word, I head out. I doubt Maddox will wake up while I'm gone. I head for the stairs, taking them to the laundry room. If anyone is in there, I guess they're getting high with me because I don't give a shit.

Fresh and dirty laundry fills the air as I enter the laundry room. But fortunate for me, it's empty. No one to pester me as I get high. There's something about hanging out in this room that almost calms me without lighting the joint, almost being the keyword. Spinning the joint between my fingers, I recall a conversation between Atticus and me when we were still in high school.

Ace takes a puff of the joint before holding it out for me to take.

The thing about Atticus is he buries his emotions. He's been this way since we were little kids when the sperm donor walked away from us. It's hard to break the shell that he carries. I've tried breaking the doors down, but it's useless. No one can get through to him.

"Pass it here and shut up. What's pissing you off, anyway?"

He leans back in the seat on the boat I randomly bought; that's what happens when I'm fuckin' high as a kit. Random ass purchases. I also lost my spending cash since.

"Jinx is what's pissing me off." He stares at the cloudy sky and sighs. Atticus sighing is never a good thing.

"Why? Got a hard-on for stepsis?" I shoot him a knowing grin. He can't keep that to himself. It's hard when he stares at her constantly.

"I swear she does shit just to piss me off. Do you believe someone stole her cello, or do you think she wanted us to get into trouble?"

I think he's lost his goddamn mind. Jinx is not conniving for one thing, and secondly, I've heard all the girls in that school hate Jinx for some reason. So, I believe that they did steal her cello. The bitches in this school are insane. I hate high school. I can't wait to leave.

"Ace, you're getting insane again. You've seen everyone in that school. Trust me, she isn't lying. What is this really about?"

"I shouldn't have made that stupid bargain with her. But I also can't let her walk away."

"So, what, you lay claim on her, and that's that?"

Amusement flickered in his eyes. "I know you want her. I'm sure Maddox does, too. I don't mind sharing. But I swear to the devil himself that if anyone touches her first, I will kill them."

"And how do you think you'll stop that from happening? We're going to different colleges."

He never told me how he would keep it from happening, and honestly, I never wanted to know. Jinx and Atticus' relationship has always been rocky. It's one thing I never understood. That's why I think he fucked it up again if she isn't talking to us, but why punish Maddox and me? We didn't do dickshit.

Maddox is going to need her more than anything.

Five

Jinx

The downfall of hiring a new dean is that he doesn't want the secretary's help settling in. Instead, he has called me more times than I can count. I don't want to step foot into Dad's old office. I can still picture Dad's slumped body on the desk and the pool of blood on the floor. I'll never be able to sleep at night wondering where his heart is and why someone took it.

I take a few deep inhales before pushing open the door for the school office. Florence is typing away on her computer, too busy to notice. Like always. I walk into the light, casting a shadow over her.

She lifts her gaze, hesitating. "Odette, so glad you made it in." She turns to look down the hall. "Allan has been antsy all morning. It's good you came in."

"In a way, I need the distraction, but I don't want to be here." I rub my chest, trying to calm the nerves.

She swivels out of her seat, moving swiftly to my side. "Sweetheart, it'll be alright. No one is asking you to move mountains." Taking my hands into hers, she squeezes them. "But I do want to warn you, that office doesn't look anything as it did. It was a shock. Prepare yourself."

"Thanks, Florence, but I don't think I'll ever be prepared to go into that office again," I tell her, blinking back tears as memories try to break through.

She wipes away a tear. "I'll be out here if you need me. There's also one more thing I need to tell you." She bites her lip, squeezing my hand tighter.

"What is it, Florence?"

"It's about Maddox." She backs away, rounding her desk, and grabs a piece of paper. "Here, this is all I know."

My hand shakes as I take the paper; what's happening with Maddox? I read over Florence's handwritten notes—no doubt from her eavesdropping. I can't believe what I'm reading; there is no way Maddox would do any of this.

Malicious mischief, breaking and entering a car, not reporting an accident. What was he thinking? This doesn't sound like him at all.

I'm going to hate asking this. "Who's car?"

"Professor Vons."

Fuck. Maddox, what the fuck were you thinking. I read the last words on the paper—criminal charges.

"Von wants to press charges?"

She nods. "Seems so. What are you going to do?"

"Where is he now?"

"Last I heard resting at home, his face is beaten up. He doesn't want to be seen at school."

It's more like he doesn't want Lula to see his mangled face. Let's add one more thing to my growing pile of shit to get through this year.

"I'll handle it, don't worry. Thanks." The pounding in my head intensifies the more I think about the situation. And I still have to help Allan. I'm not going to make it through the day at this rate.

I don't know much about Allan except he would be the perfect person to take over for Dad. I'm glad the meeting is over because I never want to hire another dean again.

If you look hard enough around this school, ravens are hidden everywhere. That's one reason I think Edgar was meant to be mine; this school works mysteriously. I pause on the raven handle when I reach the black office doors. Am I prepared to walk into this room? Absolutely not.

With a quick knock, I push open the doors. Allan is standing before the window with his hands on his hips. I clear my throat.

"Allan? It's Odette."

"I'm aware." His tone was stern, ensuring he knew who was in charge of this room.

Allan is also a cocky asshole. But I'm the one who holds all the power in this room, and I can fire him at the drop of a hat.

"Can we get this shit over with? I don't wanna be here."

He spins around, the sun casting a dark shadow over him. "Must I remind you that you are a student in this school, and you shall show me respect. Don't think you are above anyone, Miss Hawthorne."

"And I'll remind you, Allan." I walk closer to him, getting a clear view of his face. "You could've easily had Florence help you with anything that involves the school, but you chose to bring in a student."

His lip curls, pulling his mustache higher. "Are you going to be causing problems for me?"

"I'll make a deal with you, Allan. Don't cause issues for my friends or me. And I won't cause issues for you."

This is my next best thing if I can't pursue Von not to press charges. Getting Allan to be my new best bud is my saving grace. And if that involves putting him in his place, that would be even better. I'm in a fighting mood.

"Is that a threat?" He creeps forward, towering over me.

"If push comes to shove, Allan." Every time I mention his name, I watch his left eye twitch.

He snaps his fingers, pointing to his desk. "Move. I need a rundown of this school and how it functions, and then we can discuss other things."

It's the other things that I'm worried about. What if Allan doesn't want to help Maddox? I'll be doubled screwed. Allan has no idea who Maddox is. This isn't Maddox. What the hell got into him to act out? I don't understand how Dad always got the guys out of hot water. How am I going to do this? I need to channel my inner Prescott. He must've pulled so many strings, or everyone loved him to bend over backward. I don't have that kind of pull.

Allan is too cocky to let a woman tell him what to do, even if said woman is his boss. My gut is telling me he won't be helping me any. And I would rather spend my morning anywhere but in this office.

It's been three hours, and I'm elbow deep in paperwork. At this rate, Allan will never figure anything out. He keeps interrupting me while I try to explain the most straightforward thing, but he blows his top when I tell him he can't change how the school is run. We have policies in place for a reason. The only thing he is here for is to enforce the rules and keep the students in line. The board members take care of the rest. But he doesn't like my answers and throws a tantrum like a toddler. I'm half tempted to leave.

"Will you shut the fuck up, Allan. I'm not going to explain this again." My skin grows hot the more I yell at him.

"Don't you raise your voice at me, girl. I'm in charge here."

My head snaps in his direction. "I'm sorry. Whose name is on your fucking paycheck? Sit the fuck down. Jesus fucking Christ." I thread my fingers in my hair, pulling at my roots. My head pounds even worse now. "I'll explain it once more. The swim team is invaluable. You can't cut their budget. You have no authority. If you bring it up once more, I'll fire you. This school loves their Odin's Raven's swimmers."

He fixes his eyes on me, gritting his teeth. "Fine. This doesn't mean you win. I'll find something in this school to cut."

"Doubt it. You realize it's for the elites, right? You know what that means, correct?"

We're gifted, you dumbass.

"Make the call and help Maddox. Tell Von to pull his head out of his ass and stop sleeping with students, or that goes on his record. I'm not playing anymore. He smartens up, or he's fuckin' fired."

Allan hovers over the phone, fingers twitching. What the hell is he waiting for?

"Who is this Maddox guy to you?"

A fluttery feeling slams into my stomach when I think of Maddox. Once you overcome his walls, a beautiful soul is there waiting. He needs reminders that he's loved and not a broken child anymore. No one can hurt him.

"Maddox is someone you should be afraid of, now make the fuckin call."

Maddox will also ruin your entire life if you fuck with what's his.

Allan picks up the receiver, rolling his eyes. "You pray this works."

You have no idea how much I'm praying to fuckin Lucy right now. Because if Maddox goes to jail, I'm not sure what I'm going to do. Or what Ashton or Atticus will do. I'm more worried about what they have planned. Because if I know Atticus, he's already cooking up a scheme, and it will go south.

I should've just made a house call to Von and made a face-to-face conversation, but knowing Von, he would've charged me with trespassing or some stupid bullshit.

"No answer. I'll have to try later," Allan says, hanging up the phone.

"You better. I'm leaving. I have better shit to do than hang out here with you."

I leave before he says something stupid. I wave good-bye to Florence as I walk past her; I need to leave this office.

"Jinx the fucking minx."

Those words, that voice. He can't be here. He's supposed to be gone for weeks. How the hell did he get back in?

"Speechless? Did you miss me that much?" Cam asked with a curl to his lip.

I try to swallow the lump forming in my throat, but it's thick. It's choking me. I need air. Where's my inhaler? I shakily pat my fanny pack down, never taking my eyes off Cameron.

"Oh, come on, Jinx. Don't be like that." He moves closer, pushing me closer to the wall. "I missed the way you feel."

I finally get my pack unzipped, wrapping my hands around my inhaler. I shove it in Cam's face, pressing the canister until it sprays him. He stumbles away from me, grabbing his face.

"You bitch, that burns!" He screams.

I hastily take a puff, reliving my screaming lungs. "Yeah, I know, asshole," I gasp. "Touch me again, and it'll be worse."

I back away, watching him until I reach the main doors. When I feel the sun on my back, I take off and go down the path to the dorm.

What the fuck is going on at this school?

Six

Atticus

There isn't anything worse than having your best friend fucked up but having your girlfriend ignoring you—again. I swear it's a weekly thing with Jinx. But it shouldn't surprise me; she's always been like this, and I know after a few days, she'll be crawling back like nothing has happened. But I also know she's been under a lot of stress these last few weeks.

I have a solution for that if she only fucking talked to me.

I swear if I catch her, her ass is getting it. I don't fucking care at this point. I'm done with her shit. With what Maddox did, I need some stress relief. I don't know what she's up to or where she is. It's like she doesn't care that her stalker is still out there following her around.

Maddox is still passed out, so I step into the hall, pull out a smoke, and place it between my lips as I take the stairs to the exit. We all have our vices, and I'll never give mine up. The afternoon sun damn near blinds me as I light my smoke. It would be nice if the dorm were for smokers; just give me a corner. Who gives a shit if you're allergic to smoke, die for all I care. Why should I have to come outside like a dog?

I'm scanning the school grounds when I see a familiar figure running. What in the fuck? I drop my smoke, step on it to ensure it's out, and take off after her. So many scenarios are running through my head, but they don't matter. I'm getting some answers out of her, and I'm getting something for myself, too.

When I reach her, we are close to the woods—her least favorite place.

"Jinx, I'm coming for you." She turns to see me before I grab her by the waist, and she lets out a sharp scream. "Don't bother. No one will save you."

I haul her over my shoulder and move further into the woods, with her kicking and scratching me.

"Fucking let go of me, Atticus. I'm not kidding. I'll hurt you and not feel sorry for it."

"Good, that's what I want. Fight me. I need it."

She tears open my arm, blood pooling where her nails dug in, and a rush of arousal shoots to my dick, getting me hard. This is precisely what I needed, a fight. I need her to know what she does to me. I toss her on the ground, watching her tumble into a pile of leaves. When she looks at me, her hair is a tangled mess. My beautiful, tangled mess.

"I fucking hate you. I don't want anything to do with you. Haven't you figured that out yet, Atticus?"

I chuckle under my breath. I've known that Jinx hates me for a while, but she always comes back to me.

I drop to my knees, grabbing her ankles. "I know, Little Grim. Trust me, but I don't care how much you hate me; you're still going to be screaming my name, and that's all that matters." I pull her close, spreading her legs wide. I love it when she wears skirts. Jinx tries to kick my hands off her, but I only tighten my grip.

"Let go of me," she demands bitterly.

With a quirk whirl, I turn Jinx onto her stomach. Sitting on her legs, I flip her skirt up and smack her ass.

"You need to learn one thing. You aren't the boss of me." I slip my finger in between her thong, grazing her ass cheek. "Maybe we should play a game instead." She tries to wiggle free, but I only add more pressure to her legs.

"The only game you're going to play is how to eat food from a straw after I break your jaw."

So, she does know how to fight back. It's about time she found her words, not that it'll do her any good.

"I'll let you go on the count of three. You remember this game, right?"

"Fuck you," she spits out.

"Good. I'll chase, and if I catch, you're all mine, Little Grim." I smack her ass once more before pushing upward. "One."

I back away, giving her space to get up. "Two. I suggest you start moving, or I'll fuck you on the spot."

She climbs onto all fours and pushes herself up. When she turns around, her clothes are filthy. Her eyes harden as she steps back.

"I hope you trip and fall, you asshole." She swings around and takes off.

I watch as she zig-zags between trees. When she's almost out of sight, I race after her. I want her deep in the woods where no one can hear her scream, and we're alone.

"Better start running faster, Little Grim. I'm almost on your tail," I taunt her from behind.

She cranks her head back, only now realizing how close I am. Fear flickers in her eyes the closer I get. It's like Jinx only now realized she wasn't getting out of this mess. I reach out, treading my fingers in her hair, pulling tight, and snapping her head back. With a crash, she lands in my chest.

"Caught you, Little Grim. You know what that means, don't you?"

"Yeah, I'm going to knee you in the balls."

She turns and drives her knee into my balls, making me grip her hair harder until she whimpers.

"You also forget. I don't mind the pain." I reach under her skirt, push past her thong, and drive two fingers into her.

"Atticus." Her voice strains to say anything further as I pump faster.

"I know you can take it, don't fight it. Spread your legs for me." I let go of her hair to undo my pants, stroking my stiff tattooed dick. I withdraw my fingers from her, reaching up; I push on her back, bending her over. Sliding my hand down her arm, I twist her arm behind her back before slamming into her pussy. Her scream echoes in the woods.

"Fuck, Jinx. I'll never get tired of this."

She gasps the more I demand from her; with each drive of my hips, her muscles squeeze me tighter. Jinx can lie all she wants, but she loves this as much as I do. She moves her hand to the tree before us and pushes back into me.

"I fuckin' hate you, Atticus Banks." She moans.

"Yeah, I'm sure you do." I find her clit, giving it a hard pinch as she comes all over my hand. "God, I love it when you make us wet like this." Taking my wet fingers, I lean forward and press them to her lips, and she opens, willing to suck them clean.

Releasing her arm, I move back. "Get on your knees and face me."

When she turns around, she breathes hard but drops to her knees. Without being told, she opens her mouth. I cradle the back of her head and slowly slide into her mouth. I don't stop until she gags, pulling back a bit. I drive in, feeling her tongue press against my tip makes me want to explode.

"You're gonna swallow it all. Get ready." I hold her head still as I move back and forth. Pleasure takes over as I spill down her throat. "Fuck, Odette." I slip out of her mouth, and I watch her swallow all my cum.

She slumps onto her heels, looking tired. Maybe if I were a different guy, I would've asked how her day was before fucking her, but that isn't me. Small talk before isn't what I want. She has Maddox or Ashton for that shit. But looking at her now, I can tell something happened.

"Jinx?" I sink to my knees, cupping her chin. "Why weren't you with one of the guys earlier?"

She jerks her head out of my hold. "Atticus, I don't trust you."

Her words made my blood boil. How doesn't she trust me? I've been with her through everything, and now she's spouting this bullshit, not having it.

"What's going on? And don't say 'I don't know.'"

"Every time my stalker contacts me, it's always after you are around me," she mumbles, keeping her eyes downcast.

"What the fuck does that mean?"

She digs around in her fanny pack, taking out her inhaler. "I didn't stutter. What does it sound like I meant?" She takes a puff before placing it back in her pack.

"You can't honestly think I would stalk you. What would I get out of it when I've had you this entire fucking time? You forgot that valuable piece of information, haven't you? You've been mine since I moved into your house years ago. Now tell me what is going on."

With a somber expression, she looks up at me. "Cameron is back."

Rage rolls through my veins. How can that asshole be allowed back into this school? He hasn't even been gone for two weeks. What bullshit is going on here?

"What did he do to you?"

"Nothing, leave it alone." She shrugs, getting up. "Can I go? I need to get cleaned up."

"You can avoid this forever, Jinx. Having Cameron back will only bring back nightmares. You have to deal with this now."

She looks at me with defeat. "Atticus, I need a break. When do I get a break? I can't do this anymore." Tears pooled in the corner of her eyes.

Aw fuck.

I lift her into my arms, cradling her head into my neck. "Come, I'll take you back. There's someone else that needs you, too."

Even though I want to be selfish and keep her to myself, Maddox needs her. Maddox is going to be needing us all now. I'm not sure I can rescue him from this one. And I feel useless. I've been there whenever he needed me, and I'm failing him.

Maybe I am a little bit of an asshole and should start caring more, and now I'm failing Jinx. I should've been there for her today. The walk back to the dorms is quiet, and neither of us has the energy to comfort one another.

My only question remains, how the fuck did Cameron make it back onto campus. Who the fuck signed off on that? It has to do something with Roan. I know it. I don't trust that fucker, especially now that he's hooking up with Mother. They have to be cooking something up, but what?

"Drop me off at my dorm. I don't wanna see anyone."

"That's nice." I ignore her and take the stairs to my floor.

Maddox will enjoy a visit from her. God knows it'll calm the asshole down.

Seven

Jinx

I feel like I'm stuck in the movie *Groundhog,* where I live each day repeatedly until I figure out where I went wrong. The merry-go-round of dread never stops spinning, and I'm afraid if I jump off, I'll never recover.

After staying the night with Maddox, I called an emergency meeting with the board members. I need to sort some shit out, especially with Maddox, and now that Cam is back. That requires dealing with. His grandfather needs to answer some questions. He can't go behind my back and bring his asshole-raping grandson back into this school. Maybe I didn't express myself in the last meeting. I'll try harder today.

I carefully climb over Maddox; he hasn't moved an inch all night. I don't think he noticed that I climbed into bed with him. Ashton said he never came out of his room all day and wouldn't tell me what exactly happened for him to be in this state.

"Be safe today, Maddox. I'll be back, I promise." I kiss his forehead briefly, grabbing my pack before waking in the living room.

"Where are you off to?" Atticus says oh so fucking casually, without looking over at me. It irritates me.

I glare at the back of his head. "If you must know, to my dorm to change because I have a meeting that you peasants aren't welcome at."

Ashton chokes back a laugh.

"Don't start, or I'll drag you down too."

He raises his hands in surrender. "Hey, I wasn't going to. I'm on your side, Little Swan."

I sidestep toward the door, nodding like I'm paying attention when in all honesty, I'm counting down the time before I need my ass inside that board room. These guys don't give a shit about time management.

My foot hits the door, bringing the guy's attention to me.

"Jinx, you aren't going alone. You have a slight problem with that memory of yours. Just because you don't get text messages always doesn't mean your stalker isn't watching you. You let your guard down, and that is the minute he'll step out of the shadows."

"Thanks, Atticus. You don't think I remember; maybe you should get yourself a fucking stalker." I open the door, and without turning around, I tell him, "It's the worst thing you can imagine, living your life like you are afraid to breathe. I wouldn't wish this on anyone."

I calmly make my way upstairs. I know Atticus cares somewhere deep down; he does. His execution needs heaps of work. It's annoying how he thinks. I don't know how to care for myself. I punch in my door code and place one foot inside. My body froze instantly.

A trail of black feathers leads from the window to the bedroom, and still, my body won't move. I know only one animal in this place with those feathers, but why would there be so many? How did he get in here? I always have the window closed when I leave. What the hell is going on?

And then I hear it, the ding from an incoming text. My senses know before I dig my phone out who it's from. My legs lock into place, clenching my muscles tight. I try to focus on the window, hoping it'll distract me enough from going into full panic mode. But then another message comes in, and my heart speeds up.

Breathe in and out. That's all I gotta do.

My muscles gradually loosen up, and I feel like I have run a marathon. I grab my phone and open the messages before I can think twice about it.

Unknown: Odette, you still haven't taken my warnings to heart. Next time, it will be your bird.

I run into my bedroom and fall to the floor. A bloody bird lies in a circle of black feathers on my bed. But it isn't Edgar, thank God. With shaky fingers, I open his following message.

Unknown: Attached Image. Nice view of you and Atticus in the woods. Be careful, being the owner of an elite school, you wouldn't want this picture getting out, now, would you?

I lean over and throw up.

He was in my dorm. He broke into my dorm. My private fucking space, how was it possible? Out of the twins, I settle on Atticus, even though I want Ashton's calmness right now. I need Atticus.

"Jinx, did you change your mind?"

"H-he was in my dorm." The words barely come out.

"What do you mean, in your dorm?" I can hear Ashton asking questions before the door slams shut. "I'm running up the stairs. Where are you?"

I swallow hard, looking at the bed. "In my room."

"Don't move. I'm almost there."

I bend over, placing my head on the floor, trying to calm myself. This wasn't how this morning was supposed to go. Why can't one thing go my way for once?

"Jinx?" Atticus calls out.

"Here," I mumble. His footsteps vibrate under my fore-head the closer Atticus gets.

His hand lands on my back, yet I don't move. I still can't move.

"Jinx, what happened here? Are you hurt?" His voice trails off. "That's not."

"No, it's not Edgar." Not yet. That is, if my stalker has anything to do with it, at least.

Atticus kneels before me, lifting my face, and I have no choice but to sit up until we are eye to eye.

"Tell me what happened. You were only gone for five minutes."

I blow out my cheeks, a deep exhale. "When I stepped into my place, there were feathers everywhere. I thought for sure it was Edgar, but it didn't make any sense be-cause I always close the window." I tilt my head back, dreading telling him about the text messages. "And then, I-um got some messages on my phone."

"From him? Where's the phone now?"

I watch his jaw clench when I don't answer right away. I looked around for my phone but must have dropped it somewhere. The thought of the last message turns my stomach again. Closing my eyes, I take a deep, calming breath.

"Atticus, can we not right now? There is a dead bird on my bed, my stalker broke into my dorm, and I need to have a meeting with old ass men soon. I'm emotionally drained and don't have enough to deal with your temper."

"Okay, if that's how you wanna play." He moves back, pulling his phone out. His fingers fly over the screen. Not once does he look at me.

I can't stay in this room anymore. With shaky legs, I push myself upright. I force myself to look anywhere but the bed. What if that was Edgar? I don't know what I would've done. I make my way to the closet, mindlessly grabbing clothes.

"Jinx. Ashton and Maddox are coming up. One of them will be with you all day, don't worry about the mess. We'll take care of it. Do you need help to get dressed?"

The soft side of Atticus is rare, but it's lovely when it happens. If only it would happen when I wasn't in crisis mode.

"I'll be fine. Thanks." Still avoiding the room, I head for the bathroom. Perhaps alone time will do me some good. I need a break is what I need. The girl staring back at me in the mirror is not the same girl that started this school year. That girl had a fucking dream.

This girl is living each day like it's her last. And maybe I am. My parents are dead now. Who says I have much more time left here? It's my curse.

I toss my shirt to the floor, glancing at my selected outfit—a short black dress. Perfect. I'll need a little more.

Slipping it over my head, I slip my leggings off and peek out the bathroom door. All three guys are now crowded around my bed. Ashton looks from the corner of his eye, raising a brow. I shake my head, hoping he knows I'm fine. He nods in return before turning back.

Without a sound, I leave the comfort of the bathroom and just make it to my dresser.

"Jinx. I found your phone."

Of course, Atticus did. I open the top drawer, pulling out a pair of tights. "Find anything of interest?" I know he did. The picture of him slipping his dick into my pussy. I'm sure everyone in this school would pay money to see that. They would call him a champ, and I would be called a slut. What a wonderful world we live in.

I open my closet and find my gray cardigan and a pair of Converse.

"Don't be like that. You know what I fuckin' found. You have to take this seriously."

I swivel around fast. "Fuck you. Shoving your words down my throat every chance you get isn't helping me either. Why don't you understand that?"

"Baby, that's not what Ace means," Maddox calmly says.

I crack my neck, restraining myself from chewing Maddox's head off. He shifts from one foot to the other, waiting for me to explode. It's on the tip of my tongue, but the sight of him breaks me. His dull hazel eyes won't look at me, and there's something different that I can't quite place my finger on. I need to know what the hell went down beside him trying to kill Von.

Still staring at Maddox, I ask, "I'm leaving. Who's my bodyguard?"

"I am, Little Swan. Let's get you to your meeting. Don't wanna keep the old bastards waiting."

When Maddox does look at me, his eyes are gutted with pain. I crossed the room, pulling at his shirt until he crashed into me. His hand wrapped around my head and the other around my waist.

"If anything happened to you, Jinx. I wouldn't stay in this world a minute longer."

Shivers shoot down my back at his words. I wrap my arms around him, squeezing him tight.

"Maddox, please don't say that. This world needs you."

"It's shit without you, be careful." He tilts my chin back, placing a small kiss on my lips. "I mean it. I'm already in trouble with the law. I can't afford any more problems if I have to kill someone."

A small laugh escapes. "I'm working on that, I promise."

"I believe that. Go. I'll see you later."

I smile at Atticus, and he rolls his eyes but gives me a smirk in return. "Listen to Ash, Little Grim or else."

I flip him the middle finger as I walk out.

Bossy asshole.

Eight

Jinx

The walk to the main building is quiet. Ashton is too busy scoping out every inch. I'm trying to act naturally, as if nothing bothers me, and my body will tell me if something is wrong. And so far, nothing is wrong. Probably because Roan should be in the board room, but if he is my stalker, why is he waiting to make a move?

If it's money he wants, he can suck it. I'm not handing anything over. Stalk me forever because I won't cave.

"You can stay out here. It's a private business. Sorry," I tell Ashton when we reach the director's board room.

He shrugs and leans against the wall. "All good, yell if you need me and I'll be in there before you can blink."

I lean up on my tiptoes, placing a kiss on his lips. "Thank you." I go to turn when he grabs me.

"Not so fast. I need more." His mouth hovers over mine as his fingers trail up my thigh under my dress. "It's too bad you're wearing these." He tugs at my tights.

"Yeah, too bad."

He takes my mouth in a hot, demanding kiss, stealing my breath. I can feel his fingers dig into my thigh as the kiss grows more profound. When I think I can't take anymore, he buries his hand into my hair and moves his lips across my jaw.

"Fuck, Ashton." I push my body into him, feeling his hardness on my stomach.

"Trust me, Little Swan. I know." He nibbles my earlobe. "Best hurry up with your meeting so we can continue."

How am I supposed to concentrate now when my brain is going to be thinking of this moment? Reluctantly, I turn and push the boardroom doors open. Barnaby, Roan, and Archer all snap their heads in my direction when I step inside.

"About damn time. We've only been waiting twenty minutes," Archer snaps.

"The world doesn't revolve around you, Archer. Things came up that weren't my fault." I watch Roan when I say this, but I don't get a response from him.

Barnaby hums in response but says nothing further. He never does. I don't mind him, but we'll see how that goes after this meeting.

"Why are we all here, Miss Hawthorne?" Roan finally speaks.

"Ask Archer. It's his grandson that brings us all together once again." I sit in my seat, glaring at the asshole.

He smirks. "I don't know what you're talking about, Odette. After all, this is your school. Maybe you should keep better tabs on what's happening in it."

I jump out of my seat. "You sonofabitch, you know exactly what you did," I call out. Barnaby moves out of his seat, taking my arm.

"Take it easy. We can't have you getting into trouble, Miss Hawthorne. Archer, what did you do?" He turns his attention to Archer.

Archer leans back in his seat, clasping his hands behind his head. "I didn't do anything, ask Roan. He's been quiet this entire time," he says, unbothered.

I never thought of Roan. He could do this as torture. But he can't sign off on this without my signature or Archer's.

"Roan?" I raise a challenging brow in his direction.

"What if I did Odette? What are you going to do to me? Kick me off the board? You can't."

"What did you do?" I spat each word out around clenched teeth.

Barnaby still has a hold of me, and I'm thankful for that because I would be flying across this table and trying to scratch his eyes out. Roan pushes his seat back and slams his hands on the table. He shakes his head when he looks at me before turning around and walks to the window.

"You know, Jinx. I thought you would be different. I had hopes for you once your father was out of the picture. But you're just like him. Serena was right. You need to die, too."

"Roan!" Barnaby roared. "You need to calm down."

Archer sits up straight as if he's on high alert now. "What has gotten into you, Roan?"

"You need to leave and calm down," Barnaby tells him.

I'm still trying to wrap my mind around the words he said. He still doesn't gain anything if I die, so what would it matter? Serena needs to leave and has nothing to do with anything happening here. She's being a petty fucking cunt. If this is her trying to scare me, it isn't working.

"This meeting is over. Roan, get out. If I ever see you back on school grounds, I will not hesitate to call the cops and have you arrested. You can also tell Serena the same thing. This will always be my school. Thank you, gentlemen."

I watch Archer leave first, followed by Roan. Barnaby hesitates.

"It's okay. I have someone waiting for me. You can leave. Thank you for standing up for me."

"I cared for your father, Odette. Don't think I wouldn't do the same for you." With a nod, he leaves.

I sink back in my seat, releasing a breathy laugh. What a shit show that was. I still never got answers on how to get Maddox out of the deep-ass pickle that he is in. I might have to call another meeting and pray that Archer and Barnaby can pull some strings. I hope they hate Von just as much as I do.

"Doing okay, Little Swan?"

I laugh at Ashton's question. "No." And then I burst into tears.

"Oh, shit. I'm coming." He races across the room, grabs me out of my seat, and pulls me into his chest. "I'm here. It's going to be okay. You don't need to speak."

The weight of the world is getting too much for me to handle. Everything from this morning to now is growing heavy, and all it took was one simple question to open the damn. And now, with Cam back, that's one more issue to add.

Ashton presses me closer, and I wish there were a way for me to climb into his body. He makes me feel calm without even trying.

"Can we go back to my dorm?"

"No, it'll be mine or Maddox's. You won't be staying in yours anymore."

I pull away, raising my brows. "Excuse me?"

He pulls me back in. "Listen. Some wacko jacko broke into your place, and you expect us to let you stay there. No ma'am. Pick a boyfriend."

"You want me to choose? Between you three?"

He shrugs. "The competition isn't that hard. Atticus is an asshole, so he's out. If I'm being honest, you should stay with Maddox. He needs someone the most."

He does. We might need each other, if I'm being truthful. I have to tell myself that it's not long-term and that living with someone else isn't a bad thing. Besides, Maddox doesn't mind my cello playing. I just don't know how the entire floor will feel about it.

"Okay, Maddox's place will work. And this way, I'll be closer to everyone."

He interlocks our fingers, bringing them to his mouth and kissing my fingers. "Good, let's go."

When we arrived at the dorms, I wasn't expecting to find all my belongings already in Maddox's place. Even Edgar's treats are here. What was the point of asking me where I wanted to stay when they went behind my back and decided for me? This is what I mean about boundaries; they don't have any.

"Seriously, even my underwear?" After searching through all the drawers in my dresser that they brought down, I asked.

"Hey, what can I say? We wanted you to have all the necessities. And don't act like we haven't seen them before, Jinx." Atticus smirks.

"It's not the point. That's still my personal stuff."

Maddox comes up behind me, placing a kiss on my neck. "Sorry, baby. The black lace thong is my favorite if it makes you feel any better."

"It doesn't." I jab him in the stomach.

"Sorry, Little Swan. I knew you would pick this place, so they moved everything during your meeting."

I cringe at those words—the meeting from hell is more like it. I don't know what I would do if Barnaby weren't there. There was a lapse in judgment, for sure. Because I would've knocked Archer out and Roan, Jesus Christ, I thought for sure he was going to kill me.

"Sorry, Maddox, I never got any answers from the meeting. Something else came up and ate up all the time." I look back at him and give him a small smile.

"Hey, it's okay, it's all my fault, anyway. I was being a dumbass. I thought I was helping, but I made everything worse, as always. I need to take full responsibility for my actions. Don't worry about trying to help me." His eyes stayed fixed on an object over my head as he spoke.

"I have some plans in the works, don't worry. It'll all be resolved. I'm not letting you go to prison." I cup his cheek, bringing his attention to me. "Trust me."

I hope Allan is doing his part, too. Because if I do have to make a house call, it won't be pretty, and I won't be showing up alone this time. Why does it always take a man? I hope Allan realizes I can ruin his career alone. Having the guys there will be extra.

"Alright, love birds. We're gonna head out. Jinx, have fun with this guy, and remember you could be sleeping next to this asshole." Ashton smacks Atticus in the head.

"I'm gonna kill you," Atticus snarls back.

Maddox laughed lazily, and it was a sound I had been missing.

"Go. I'll text you guys later."

Ashton places a kiss on my lips and moves for his brother. Atticus kisses my forehead but doesn't move. His blue eyes narrow.

"You aren't telling us something, Jinx. What happened in that meeting?"

I can feel the lump rising in my throat; no matter how often I swallow, it won't go away. What am I going to say that Roan and Serena could be psychopaths?

And deep down, I don't think Roan is my stalker. What is there to say?

"Nothing happened. We're just talking about Cam, that's all. Everything is fine, Atticus."

He brushes the pad of his thumb over my bottom lip, then pinches it. "Don't lie to me."

"I'm not. That's what our meeting was about."

He tilts his head, shaking it. "You're holding something back, and I have ways of finding things out, Jinx. I wouldn't keep that secret for too long."

I watch him leave and pray that he doesn't discover what happened.

Nine

Maddox

Having Jinx stay with me is a blessing and a curse. Deep down, I know why the guys made her stay with me, and the thought turns my stomach. They only want the best for me, but using our girlfriend as a babysitter doesn't sit right with me. The worst part is I can't even escape this hell hole anymore because Jinx took my car keys. I miss having my own space and the freedom to do anything. I can only pray Jinx hasn't found my secret stash.

I still don't have any answers about what my future is like. No one will tell me. Von hasn't returned to school, and this new dean won't see me. Every time I try, Florence says he's out of the office. Which I know is complete bullshit. He doesn't want to deal with a fuck up like me. Some punk asshole was trying to kill a teacher. But in all honesty, I wasn't trying to kill Von. Maybe scare him—kill. I was trying to kill him.

The unknown is killing me. Why can't someone tell me what is happening? Going on with my life and acting like I won't be arrested any second is exhausting. I've been living on edge my entire life. All I want is a break from this feeling. My nerves are completely shot, and if I don't find something to calm me down soon, I'm going to explode. With that in mind, I ditch out on my last class, hoping no one is in my dorm room. I step off the last step of the main building only to hear my name.

"Maddox. How's it going? Still, using Jinx's pussy? Or are you done with that?"

I gradually turn around and face Cameron. If one thing is for sure, I never missed the prick. "You never learn, do you, Cam?"

He slips his hand into his front pocket and shrugs. "I'm not overly worried, wanna know why?"

I let out a long, lingering breath; I guess I can entertain him. "No, Cam. I have no idea, but I feel you're going to fill me in."

He gives a bitter laugh. "Oh, Maddox. You can't touch me, or I'll have your ass thrown in jail."

It's my turn to laugh. "I guess the warning Atticus gave you didn't sink in. I'll give you a refresher."

Before my words could sink in, I move in a blink of an eye. My fist collides with his mouth, giving me some satisfaction. The pussy dropped to his knees, head in his hands, screaming in pain. Bloody drool spills onto the grass from between his fingers.

"You'll pay for this, Maddox." He raises his face, giving me a bloody smile. "Mark my fucking word, you won't be in this school another day."

"Don't tease me, Cameron, because I would be careless if I stayed in this school for another day. Come up with a better threat." I kick Cameron to the ground. "Be grateful it wasn't Atticus you ran your mouth to. He's been going a little too easy on you."

I step over him, needing my stash more than anything. At this point, I would suck a fuckin' dick just for some pills, I wouldn't even care. I will my legs to move faster across the campus. The need to get inside my dorm grows with each step. Just thinking about popping a few pills sends tingles down my spine. I bolt through the Darrow Hall doors, damn near knocking over someone standing too close to the entrance.

"Watch it, asshole!" they yell.

"Yeah, sorry about that." I don't bother looking behind me; they need to learn not to stand by a fuckin' door. I quickly jog up the stairs, praying that no one is back. I just need them gone long enough to get high.

There is complete silence when I open my door. I don't waste time heading to the bathroom, flinging open the cupboard door. I feel under the sink until my hand touches the small plastic baggie. My heart damn near did a cartwheel as I pulled my happy pills from under the sink. The small white pills slide down my throat with ease.

A wave of calmness washes over me.

The cloud I'm floating on soars through the sky like a feather. I'm untouchable from up here. The world looks like a fun size candy bar. I could fit it in my pocket and carry it around; it's perfect. I let my hand fall free, feeling the air between my fingers. I love the freeness and will never give it up to anyone. I close my eyes and enjoy the sensation.

From a distance, I can hear my name being called, but there isn't anyone around. The more I try to look around, the blurrier my surroundings become.

"Maddox."

There's my name again. Who the fuck is calling me? And why? Before I can think, the cloud I'm on starts falling to the ground. My eyes shoot open, and my fist flies out, barely missing the person beside me.

"Maddox," Jinx spoke my name, but it's barely audible.

I might be awake, but my brain isn't functioning. Jinx is nothing but a moving blur. No matter what I do, my eyes won't focus. I blindly reach for her, and her soft hand grabs my fingers.

"I have you."

Her fingers work through my hair, sending tingles to my toes. She shouldn't be here. Why does she always seem to find me after I plummet? I open my mouth to say anything but can't form a word.

"Shh, you don't need to speak. I took care of everything for you; I promise nothing will happen to you while I'm by your side, Maddox. I fucking promise you that."

I move closer, resting my head on her thighs, and wrap my arms around her legs.

"I'm sorry, baby," I tell her, blinking a tear free.

She gently traces my scar as we sit in silence. I'll never know what I did to deserve this unforgettable person, but I thank my lucky stars every day I breathe; she's still here with me. Her gentle caresses soothe me, but it's not enough; it'll never be enough.

"Hey, pretty boy."

I bury my head deeper into my pillow. "Ashton, no. Please." I slide my hand around the bed, and the fuckin' lightbulb finally lights up. "How did I get into bed?"

"Your noble steed carried your drugged-up ass. I swear, Maddox." Ashton goes quiet.

I chance it and look at him. His pale blond hair is a tousled mess, and dark circles line under his eyes. I did that to him; he's my best friend, and I am destroying him. This isn't what friends do.

"Maddox, if you pull this shit again. I'm hauling your ass into rehab." He closes his eyes, then shakes his head.

"I'm sorry, I tried."

"Don't give me that bullshit. If you tried, you would've lasted longer than a few days. Don't you ever think of anyone other than yourself?"

His words cut deep. Because I wasn't thinking about anyone, only the fact that I needed the high. And this is why I shouldn't be walking on this planet anymore. I'm not worthy. Why can't they see that by now? Why can't they just give up on me, too?

A light tap on the door frame pulls me from my dreaded thoughts.

"Can I have a word with him, please?" Jinx walked further into the room, her face unreadable.

Ash meets her halfway, brushing his fingers over her face. "Take it easy on his ass, Little Swan." He presses a kiss on her forehead before looking at me.

"Watch your mouth with her."

The click of the door makes my stomach sink. Whatever Jinx has to say will break me. I haven't moved, and neither has she a standoff that one of us isn't going to win.

"Maddox. I'm going to speak, and you're going to listen. Do not interrupt me."

I simply nod because what else can I do?

"When I walked into this dorm earlier, I was excited to be coming home to you. I wanted to share the good news with you. Instead." She drew in a shaky breath. "I found you, and I wasn't sure if the demons were dragging you to the other side. I already lost a loved one, and I'm not about to lose another one. I will not go through that again. I need you to heal, Maddox. You can't do that at this school, not for me or the guys, but for yourself." She wipes her nose, sniffing. "Swear to me. You'll find some help."

I climb out of bed, grabbing the nightstand when the world spins. Fuck. I go to say something, but balls of sawdust get caught in my throat. I inch closer to where Jinx stands, I go to reach for her hand but change my mind.

"Odette. It was never my intention to hurt you. Everything was overwhelming me, and I needed an outlet. Do you think I enjoy you always finding me at the lowest fucking point in my life? I feel like I'll never be the man you want me to be. Why would you even want to be seen with me?" I glance her way as tears stream down her cheek. "I can't be around you without making you cry. A real man wouldn't make his woman cry. Maybe you're right. I should go away and get help. I'm doing no one any good here, and you won't be safe around me if I slip up again."

The sound of our hearts breaking is deafening. Never in my life did I think we would be standing here, falling apart.

"Maddox, if you did get help. It should be because you want it, not because we want it for you. No one can fix you but you."

"What if I can't be fixed?"

She extends a hand, and I take it. "What if it does much more?"

A cold tremor ran down my spine. Would I still be the same person? What if no one wants me around after? I'll be right back where I started. It's a never-ending circle, and I'll never find a way out. Then again, I can't keep living like this; I'm hurting everyone that I love.

My fingers dig into her hand. "I'll go."

She crushes her body against mine, locking her arms around my neck. "I'm proud of you, Maddox. We'll all be here cheering you on."

"I hope so, baby."

I have a bad feeling about leaving her behind.

Ten

Ashton

The drive to Black Orchid rehab is quiet. After Maddox and Jinx had told us what they had discussed, we devised a plan and enrolled Maddox in a two-week program. He didn't feel right leaving for anything longer, not with her stalker still out there and not knowing who killed her dad. Two weeks is better than nothing.

I never thought this would happen. I thought for sure I would've seen the signs and would've been able to step in before Maddox took a turn. As his friend, I should've been there more for him. I failed him. Now, it lands on him to heal without us.

Black Orchid reminds me of a mental hospital. The brick exterior is crumbling from the ivy that decided to take residency along the walls. The window frames are chipping away from years of sun damage. Why are we sending Mad here? This can't be a working rehab. He's going to get shock therapy in this place. Do rehabs not get funding to keep their buildings up to code anymore?

"I have a bad feeling about this place, guys."

Jinx places her hand on my thigh, giving it a gentle squeeze. "He'll be okay here. It's the closest one to us, and he can call anytime to get back to us," she said calmly, giving me a sweet smile.

"I guess. I worry, that's all." I watch Maddox. He's been staring out the passenger window the entire drive. I'm surprised he didn't fight Atticus when he demanded the car keys. Maddox doesn't let anyone drive his baby. That's how I know things are bad.

"Everyone ready?" Atticus quietly asks.

No one replies. I don't think any of us can ever truly be ready for this, especially Maddox. It's his life that's going to change the most. He's giving up a lot.

"Can I head in alone?" Maddox looks from Atticus to me and, lastly, at Jinx.

Jinx leans forward, placing her hand on Maddox's shoulder. "Of course. You do what you need to."

He reaches his hand to hers and opens his door without looking at her. "I'll see you guys in two weeks." Grabbing his bag, he leaves without saying another word.

"The fuck, that's how he's leaving us." Atticus fired off, starting the car. He slams it into gear. "Fuck him."

"Atticus, don't. It's his way of processing all of this. I know you're hurting, too. We're gonna have to stick together and be a unit. Nothing changes just because he is gone," Jinx explained.

I know she's right, but Maddox could've at least tried harder. The least he could've done was give Jinx a decent goodbye. Then again, it's Maddox we're talking about. He never did like goodbyes. I hope this rehab is what he needs and that he comes back whole.

"I didn't have the chance to explain the Von situation to him."

"It'll be worth it when he comes out, Jinx. Good news will be what he'll need," I remind her.

She leans her head on my shoulder, resting her hand on my thigh. "It's only two weeks, and everyone will survive."

"Fuckin' rights, Little Grim," Atticus says. His eyes meet mine from the rearview mirror, and then he glances at Jinx.

I gently shift her hand from my thigh as I trace mine along her stomach, gliding towards the waistband of her leggings.

"Need a distraction, Little Swan?" I dip my hand inside, inching my finger to her clit. I can feel her breath on my neck when I press against it. "Relax, don't think so much. Let me take care of you."

I make small, slow circles until her hips mock the same movement. She spreads her legs wider, a silent plea for more, and who am I to say no to her? With a little more pressure, her head rolls off my shoulder, and that sweet moan I love hearing spills from her lips.

"Ash, I need more."

I glance back at Ace, and he nods, pulling over to the side of the road.

"Alright, but it has to be fast. Lay your head in my lap." She moves into position as Atticus opens the passenger door with his jeans already unbuttoned.

"You get me, Jinx." Atticus slides his hands along her legs, dipping his fingers into the waistband of her leggings, and slips them halfway down her things. Atticus kneels on the seat, lifting her legs onto his shoulders.

"Please, Atticus. I need you."

I don't think I've ever heard those words from Jinx. She reaches her hand for my waistband but stops. When her eyes reach mine, I know what she's asking. With a deep inhale, I unzip my jeans and slip my dick out. I wrap my hand in her hair, turning her how I want her. I check out Atticus; he smacks his dick against her pussy, I shove my dick into her mouth, and Atticus slams into her.

Her throat tightens, sending shockwaves through me. I'm still not used to being touched, but if I don't think about it, my mind won't go to the darkness. I have to remind myself it's Jinx and no one else. I push her face further down until her nose touches my stomach.

"Fuck, just like that. How does it feel to have both of us inside of you at the same time?" I pull her back, watching my dick slip out of her mouth. A haze of hunger swam in her eyes.

"I think she likes it, brother." Atticus drives in deeper, moving her higher across my thigh.

Her mouth drops open, and I take the chance to shove my dick back in. Closing my eyes, I forget about everything. It's a fantasy world. There is no stalker after Jinx, and Maddox isn't in rehab. For now, I'm living in pure bliss, and nothing, I mean absolutely nothing, is wrong.

"Come for me, Little Grim, squeeze the shit out of my dick."

Jinx moans around me, and I fight the urge to spill down her throat. I slide my hand across her throat, giving it a tight squeeze, holding her in place; then I turn to Atticus and grin.

"Make her come."

He spreads her legs as wide as they can go and gives her pussy a hard smack. Her muffled scream turns to a moan when Atticus quickly thrusts into her roughly.

"Oh, shit." Ace drives in deep. "Yes, Little Grim. Just like that."

Pleasure rolls through her body, and she doesn't fight it. I roll my hips, taking my pleasure and spilling everything I have down her throat.

The car fills with silence as we take the moment to collect ourselves. Guilt tries to take over. We're out here enjoying ourselves while Maddox is now locked in that horrible place, trying to fix himself. It's not fair. How is any of this fair?

"We should get back. The coach wants to have a meeting with the team this afternoon."

"Fuck Bran, he's a dick, just like coach was. Nothing changes in this school." Atticus drops Jinx's legs and tucks himself back into his pants. We both watch him leave the back of the car like nothing.

"Here, let me help you. Ace was never good with aftercare." I button my pants up before helping Jinx up. "You okay?"

"I'm perfect, what about you?" She reaches out, cupping my cheek. "It was a lot for you, wasn't it?" She studies my face for any remorse. She leans up, pressing her lips to mine when she finds none. "Thank you, Ashton."

I narrow my brows in confusion. "For what?"

"For trusting me." She moves away, fixing her pants just as Atticus jerks open the front door.

"Ready, losers?" he asks as he starts the car.

A burst of laughter poured from me, leaning forward to punch his shoulder. "You're the only loser, drive dickhead."

Jinx laughs lightly, cuddling into my side. I haven't seen her this carefree in a while, and I would give anything to make it last. Unfortunately, it'll be gone once we cross those gates back into RWA. The stalker will be there, and we won't have Maddox. God knows what else awaits us.

If we don't figure out this stalker problem soon, it will only worsen. Breaking into her dorm is only the beginning of his derangement. I don't want to think of what he's capable of, and it's annoying how he won't tell her where her dad's heart is. The one piece that would give her closure, if that sick psycho did something to Prescott, I'll be the first person to drive a knife through his chest.

My chest sinks as we cross the gates back onto the school's property, and reality sinks in. I keep telling myself it's two weeks, and Maddox will be back. If shit gets bad, he will call for a rescue mission. One thing at a time, for now, it's a stupid swim meeting.

"Jinx, you're gonna have to come with us. I don't want you alone." I sweep a chaotic piece of hair from her face. "Don't argue, please."

"What do you expect me to do the entire time?"

Atticus snorts. "Check me out. It wouldn't be the first time. At least now you don't have to look ashamed while you do it."

Her jaw drops. "I—You. Shut up."

"Yeah, that's what I thought. Not very good with the comebacks, are ya?"

"I'm not staring at you, Atticus. Maybe I'm staring at everyone else."

He slams on the brakes, and we hit the back of the seats. He swings around, grabbing Jinx's hair and cranking her neck to the side.

"If I see you looking at another man, you'll quickly learn who you belong to. Got it?" he spoke coldly, that I even got goosebumps.

I watch the lump in her throat as she tries to swallow.

"Atticus. I swear there isn't anyone else besides the three of you."

He shoves her back and starts driving again. I knew he was possessive, but this was a little much; even then, again, I can't say much. If she even looked at someone else, I would lose my fucking mind.

Eleven

Jinx

I'll be the first to admit it, but I missed the smell of the pool. What I didn't miss was Cameron. I was stupid thinking he wouldn't be here; obviously, he would be. He's the captain. When the guys turn their backs to me, Cam glances at me and licks his lips. It takes everything in me not to throw up. He would never be back in this school if it weren't for his grandfather. I would make it so that even community college wouldn't even accept his ass.

But my torture fest isn't over, and whatever Cam has planned is only the beginning. His face needs to be beaten again. I wish Maddox were here, and then I wouldn't have to endure this kind of torment. Cam looks away when Ash turns to me. He tosses Cam a side-eye; his eyes burn with fury when he looks back at me. I shake my head to reassure him nothing happened.

I watch everyone get a lecture from the new captain. It turns out that the team isn't training how they should be. It's entertaining to watch a bunch of twenty-year-olds getting their asses reamed out. I didn't know everyone was slacking on getting into a pool. I should've known Ashton and Atticus hadn't been here since Dad had died. I took them away from the one thing that kept them at the school.

I dig in my fanny pack for my phone; the guys won't notice if I secretly take a photo of them or maybe two. As I take the picture, Atticus looks over his shoulder; his eyes seem radiant with pleasure, but no. Not Atticus; that radiant glow is something else.

My phone dings, making me jump.

Unknown: My sweet Odette. Don't you want to know where your father's heart is?

My heart bottoms out; this has been on my mind since I found Dad in his office with the hole in his chest. I still don't know why someone would want to remove his heart.

Me: What do you want in return?

Unknown: You'll find out when you find the heart. Do we have a deal?

Fuck. I must be stupid because my brain says take the deal, and so does my heart. My stomach isn't saying anything. I don't think anyone understands why it's so important that I recover Dad's heart. I still can't comprehend why the cops can't do their fucking job and search for his killer. We all know a student didn't do this. It had to be Serena and Roan. That's the only possibility, and I just can't figure out why. I swear when I find out, I'll kill them myself.

Me: You have a deal, but we do this now.

Unknown: Good girl, meet me in the basement in twenty

Unknown: Alone, Odette. Don't even think about letting them know

That means sneaking out, which is one thing I'm not good at. I watch the guys waiting for the perfect time to make my escape. When their backs are turned, I make my way down the bleachers.

My foot barely makes it on the tiles when Atticus yells at me, "Where are you going? Little Grim."

Heat creeps up my cheeks, but I refuse to face the crowd behind me. One look at me, and Atticus will know I'm lying.

"My asthma is acting up; I need some air. I'll be in the lady's room." I don't like pulling the asthma card, but with desperate times.

"Want me to go with you?" Ashton asks with concern laced in his voice.

"Uh, no. I'm fine." I cringe when I don't sound convincing. I need to leave before they come over here.

I dart out of the aquatic center until I reach the main doors. I don't have time to waste; the basement is on the main campus, and I've already wasted enough time. *Unknown* never told me what would happen if I was late; honestly, I don't want to find out. His messages have been getting more intense, and to break into my dorm, he's capable of anything. Yet here I am, running head first into the fucking basement of the school, and didn't ask any questions.

The basement has always been where I never wanted to go, nothing good happens in cold, dark places. I'm hoping *Unknown* isn't down there, that he left Dad's heart, and that'll be the end of this journey. I stroll into the main campus and avoid the route to the office. If Florence or Allan saw me, there would be many suspicions. Taking the stairs to the lower level, where the staff lounge and the nurse's office are found, I follow the brick to the end. The basement entrance is just around the corner, and I swear my body grows colder with each step.

I check the time from his last text, and my body tenses when I notice I have five minutes to spare. That's all to determine if I'm in or out. Will this asshole finally be finished with his emotional torture on me, or does he have more planned? I only want him to answer why he picked me.

I unzip my fanny pack and find my inhaler, letting out an extended swoosh of air. I fill my lungs with that sweet medication. There's no way I'm getting caught having an attack if I need to run; squeezing my inhaler, I round the corner and face the basement door.

The large wooden door should belong in a medieval castle. The oak hasn't been restored, slowly fading yearly; the large black metal hinges keep it all together. The only new thing on this door is the deadbolt. Honestly, if someone wanted to get down there, all you would need is an axe.

I pull the handle, and the door creaks open. Darkness waits for me. Am I doing this? Jesus Christ, I am.

I take my first step when I remember that my phone has that stupid flashlight feature. The further I descend, the colder the air becomes; the brick walls are shiny with mildew, and the smell of mold and earth takes hold of me—the stairs round coming to a large open room. I shine the light around, and a sense of dread creeps in when three hallways appear. How the hell am I supposed to know where to go?

I feel like one of those chicks in a horror movie because I'm about to do something stupid.

"Hello?" My voice echoes off the walls. I take the last step onto the dirt floor, listening for any sound. "You better be down here."

I move to the middle, wondering which hall to pick. Or if I should say fuck it and leave. My phone dings in my hand, scaring the shit out of me.

Unknown: The middle hallway

I'm smarter than this, aren't I? I glance at the hall; I guess not—anything for you, Dad. I squeeze my inhaler tighter and take slow steps, and if the cult rumors are true, I wonder where their little hideout is. What the hell did they use this basement for, anyway? I pass one door to my left and pray that *Unknown* won't jump out; hell, he can do it for all I know. I have no clue where this path goes. Why didn't I call Spencer?

Unknown: There's an open door on the right, enter it

I like how he gets to make all the rules. The beating of my heart grows louder with each step. A yellow glow shines from a few feet ahead, and this is my chance to turn around; in doing so, I'll never recover Dad's heart. I'm stuck between a rock and a hard spot. I look behind me; freedom lies that way, and so do the twins.

Shit, the twins. They probably already figured out that I'm not coming back. Maybe it's not freedom after all. My ass will be reamed out like there's no tomorrow. I might as well do it with a heart in my hand. I take slow, steady steps. I'm in no hurry. What is *Unknown* gonna do? Leave? I'm already down here, plus he didn't say I couldn't take my time. All I had to do was be down here in twenty. Found a loophole.

Unknown: Hurry up, I don't have all day. And I'm sure those boyfriends of yours will be looking for you by now

News flash, asshole, I'm standing at the fucking door. I just don't have the balls to walk in.

"Odette, you need to hurry. School starts soon, and we're going to be late."

"I'm coming, Daddy." I climb down the stairs in the pink dress I picked out the night before. When Daddy sees me, he looks sad. "What's wrong? Why are you crying?"

He kneels in front of me, running his hand through my hair. "Oh, pumpkin. I'm not sad. I'm happy. Today is a big day for both of us. It's the start of endless possibilities. You, my sweet girl, are going places, and I can't wait to see."

"Daddy, it's only kindergarten." I giggle.

"You wait and see. I love you with all my heart."

With all his heart, that's the push I need to walk into this room. I take a deep breath and move in front of the open door. The yellow light that's been shining is nothing but an old lamp sitting on a stack of books in the corner.

I hesitantly step inside, praying I'm not about to get jumped. But rational Jinx is gone when I see a box positioned on a stool in the middle of the small room; I don't think I bolt toward it like my ass is on fire. Pain grips my chest as I reach for the box.

"Not so fast," a deep robotic voice says behind me. "I told you, I want something in return."

As I turn around, I suddenly see my stalker standing before me. My whole body freezes with fear as he takes a step closer, cutting off any chance of escape. His eyes look so eerie when they meet mine, especially with his hood covering most of his face and casting scary shadows.

I swallow the nausea that's creeping into my throat; whatever he wants can't be good. "What is it?"

He digs into his black cargo pants pocket, pulling out a key. "This will open that box under one condition." He steps closer, and my heart tightens with fear; being this close to my stalker, I'm too afraid to try anything. I grip my inhaler when he stops in front of me. "I want you to leave this school, Odette."

My mind goes blank, that's all. He's been tormenting me for months for that. Leave my school. He has got to be kidding me. What the fuck for? I turn back to the box.

"How do I know my dad's heart is in there?"

He laughs with that creepy, distorted voice. "You don't, that's the point. I need an answer."

The longer I gaze at the box, the more I'm convinced I can hear Dad's heartbeat. The fact that he's still here is such a comforting presence. But I still need to get him out of the basement. I reach out and trace my finger along the lock.

"You can't keep him forever, you know. You have no right to him."

"I know." His breath tickled the side of my neck. I go to move when his arm wraps around my waist. "I can't let you run. You should've agreed with me."

A sharp prick to the side of my neck made me lose my breath. Did he just inject me with something? I attempt to rub my neck as though something has bitten me, but my movements are sluggish, and everything's getting fuzzy around the edges. My head rolls forward, and my knees buckle.

The guys are gonna be pissed with me, is the last thought rolling through my head.

Twelve

Atticus

I'll murder her.

Went to the restroom, my ass. I couldn't concentrate the entire swim practice, and it didn't help that Cameron kept running his fucking mouth. If Bran weren't watching so closely, I would've drowned the asshole. He kept going like Ash and I weren't there, even in the change room. I had to hold Ash back a few times, but I told him when Mad is back, we'll have our fun. Cameron will be finished for good.

My main concern is finding that God-forsaken girl-friend. Each call rings before heading to voicemail. We should have activated her location, and with each passing minute, my anxiety shoots through the roof.

Ashton went to look inside Darrow Hall while I headed to the main campus. The only way she could've left the property is with Spence or if someone dragged her out. I'm hoping it's neither, to be honest. It's not that I care if she hangs with Spence, but she would've told us, and that's what is bugging me. Fuck it.

Me: Is Jinx with you?

Beats wondering and making me go any crazier than I already am.

Dickhead Spencer: No. I've been in class all day

Me: Okay, thanks

I Ignore the text he sends after. He's useless to me now. It still leaves unanswered questions. Where the fuck is Jinx? And I can't ask anyone else since Miss Darkness didn't make any other friends. It's like looking for a needle in a haystack. Fuck the main campus; I veer for Greywood Hall. Maybe she's practicing her Cello. I'm praying fucking hard that's where she is. Why can't she fucking listen to us? All Ash asked was to be with us during the meeting. How hard is that?

I'm beyond pissed, and red has now become my favorite color. I pity anyone who gets in my way, including this prick who's walking slowly in front of me. Without thinking, I give him a shove and watch him tumble to the ground.

"You asshole!" he yells at me.

I stop and swivel around. "I wouldn't start with me, or you won't use your mouth to eat from."

He doesn't say anything else. It's probably the smartest thing he's done his whole life. I continue moving, weaving in and out of all the dicks of this pathetic school. I'm trying not to think the worst, but I can't help it. What if her stalker caught her, or Serena somehow convinced her to sign the school over. Then there is that ass Roan. How has she built a fan base of haters?

The music hall is chaotic. Finding her here will be a challenge. With each person that passes by, my patience wears thin. As my phone vibrates in my pocket, I desperately hope it's Ashton with good news.

"Ash, tell me something, bother."

"Nothing, man. She isn't in Maddox, ours, or her dorm. I even checked the laundry and common area. She isn't here. Any luck on your end?"

"Wish I could say I had good news, but nothing. I'm at the music hall, trying to find her, but I'm getting pissed off." I bump into another dickhead, trying to make my way to a classroom.

I hear Ash sigh. "Breath, dude. I'll be over there shortly."

The line goes dead. I push further in, still coming up empty-handed. When I reached the concert hall, my temper maxed out. I shove the doors open and find it empty.

I breathe deeply and settle into a vacant seat, letting my head rest in my hands as my thoughts drift to where Jinx might be. I would say her ignoring us isn't like her, but her track record speaks for itself.

I swear if this is her way of just avoiding us, she wins. I'll give her what she wants. I'll drop out and move. I can't keep up with her mood swings anymore. I'm emotionally wrecked. The worst part is we can't tell Maddox. He needs to stay in rehab for the entire time. This would send him spirally to the finish line. Fuck, Maddox. We only dropped him off this morning; it feels like days have passed. If he finds out, he'll be broken. We need to find Jinx before that happens.

I try Jinx once more; this time, her phone goes directly to voicemail. My stomach sinks, and now my mind runs freely in the wind. Either her phone died, or she got sick of me blowing it up and turned it off.

"Ace. If you think any harder, you'll blow a blood vessel. We'll find her." Ash says from behind me.

I glance over my shoulder and take in a disheveled Ash. "You don't know that. We've always been able to find her. Something is different this time."

He rests his hand on my shoulder, squeezing it. "We'll find her. Did you check the main campus?"

"No, I needed a breather." I need more than a breather, but Jinx is my priority now. I'm at a loss, and I'm feeling useless. "Do you know anyone that can track a person?"

He goes to answer, then stops. He pulls his phone out and types. I watch his eyebrows furrow with each movement of his fingers. Whatever he's writing, he's making his point known. I hope whoever is on the other end doesn't fuck this up because I'm out of options. A person can't disappear without a trace. It's not possible.

"Okay, I sent a text to my nerd. Let's fucking pray he knows how to figure something out."

His fucking nerd. "Seriously, you're banking on the hope that he can find our girl, but you don't even know if he can. I've known you to do stupid shit, but this tops it, Ashton. I'm headed to the main building while you wait for your prayers to be answered."

Jesus, a nerd, to find Jinx, he has to be kidding. Nerds are only good for one thing. To cheat from or to beat up. They can't find people—end of story. What's next? He's going to ask a bookworm to find her; maybe a fictional character can hack into the school and find her. Shit doesn't happen like that in the real world. Sometimes, we only have what we have to work with, and I have nothing.

I storm out of Greywood Hall. My last hope stands in the final building with two other people who talk to her. If they haven't seen her. I'm officially fucked. Walking up the stairs, a sense of dread washes over me. She was here; I know it. Florence better have some answers. It's better than a fuckin' nerd.

The office is busy; I guess most of these dicks are trying to figure out their schedules as they try to leave for Thanksgiving next weekend. But that isn't my problem; besides them getting fat from overcooked pies, I have more important things to deal with. Florence glances my way, looking tired, and I simply nod with understanding.

I whistle, grabbing everyone's attention. "Hey. The office is closed. Get your shit and leave."

"Who made you the boss?" A curly-haired prick asked.

I step up to him, towering over him. I look into his eyes, watching him shrink down. "The knife in my back pocket did. Would you like to feel it going into your chest?"

His Adam's apple bobs up and down as he tries to swallow. I jerk forward, watching him stumble backward. He grabs his friend, and they scramble. When I reach behind my back, the rest of the crowd rushes out.

"Atticus, that wasn't necessary," Florence scolds me.

"Sure it was. I needed your help, and it looked like you needed a break." I move toward the desk, leaning on it.

"It looks like you need a break, hun. What's the matter?"

I close my eyes and take a deep breath. When I open them, Florence is watching me patiently. She's one person here who has never been rude or judged me for all my tattoos. She's always been so accepting; now, if I ask her about Jinx, she hasn't seen her. It'll break her. I'm unsure what to do: protect her or risk it.

"Have you seen Jinx today?" Jinx is more important to me. I'll risk anyone at this point.

Her face scrounges up as she thinks. "No. She usually visits, but not today. She must've gotten busy."

"Allan didn't have a meeting with her?" I'm pulling at strings now; she would've told us if she did, but I'm desperate for an answer.

"No. Allan is away for a conference in the city. He won't be back until Monday. What's going on?"

"I have a feeling Jinx is missing."

"Missing? What the hell is going on, Atticus."

Is it my place to tell her about Jinx's stalker? Jinx had plenty of time to tell her dad and never did. He could've helped her, and now it's too late. She needs help, and I won't let that pass by. I'm tired of keeping secrets. I've kept her a secret for years, and it's tiring.

"Jinx has a stalker, Florence. I'm not sure if he finally caught up with her or if she left the school grounds alone. But I need to find her."

She gently leans back in her chair, removing her glasses and letting them rest on her chest, held in place by a delicate chain. "Atticus," she whispers. "Why didn't you tell me this beforehand? Or even when Prescott was still alive, we could've helped her. What if." She broke into a quiet cry.

"Florence, I don't want to think of the what-ifs. Because if I do, I'll go to a very dark place."

"I wish I knew where she was, but I don't. I wouldn't even know where to look. I'm sorry."

I'm back at square one. With no other clues to go on, I've got nothing. I'm unsure what to do if Jinx doesn't contact me.

Thirteen

Maddox

Five days in this shitty hell hole. Five days without a drop of alcohol or a pill sliding down my throat. I wanna say it's been sunshine and rainbows, but it's like burning in hell. No matter how much I beg and plead, no one here gives a fuck. They probably wouldn't throw a bucket of water on me if I were on fire. I don't know what I was thinking; I need to get out of here.

I thought it would be easy to sneak out, but guards walk the halls at night looking for the troubled residents. That would be me and the one person I befriended in here. Wilde. He's been stuck in this shit box for two months, and he said there is only one way out besides getting signed out. I'm banking on his exit because I need to leave, and I know he does, too. They can't keep us in this place against our will.

"Yo, Maddy, are we doing this or what?" Wilde comes strolling into my room, pulling his copper hair into a bun.

I grab my bag off the stained mattress that this lovely facility provides. Wilde grins at me. He's in here to detox off heroin. That's one drug I don't wanna touch, especially after some of the stories he's told me. But I'm glad he's still standing here today.

"Yeah, let's get the fuck out of here; if I stay here one more minute, I'll blow."

Wilde peeks his head into the hall and gives me a thumbs-up. I have no idea what his plan is, but I trust him. The staff are all chatting at the reception station, and I hope they stay distracted as we take off in the opposite direction toward the stairs.

"Be quick once this door opens; the goal is the laundry room. Don't stop until we get there." Wilde pulls a card from his back pocket. "Ready?" He looks over his shoulder, and his green eyes light up joyfully.

"More than anything."

He taps the card on the card reader, and the light turns green, and the door unlocks. He pushes the door open and takes off down the stairs. I follow without thinking. My heart jumps out of my chest the further we get; whatever Wilde has planned, I hope it works out because I

can't stay here another minute. I know I promised everyone that I would get sober, but not here. This place is
worse than anything I've ever experienced before.

Wilde slips on the last step, rounding the corner, and
chuckles. "What a rush, hey, Maddy?"

"You have no idea, but I'll feel better once we're out."

"Soon, I promise."

We run down a narrow hall, stopping at the last door
on the right—the laundry room. Wilde knocks three
times, and the door opens. An older woman dressed in
navy scrubs waves us in.

"Hurry, the truck will be here soon. You don't have
much time." She pulls a large industrial-size laundry bin
over and moves sheets out of the way.

I stare at her in disbelief. "You want us to get in there
with dirty laundry?"

She rolls her eyes, "It's clean, now hurry. You're wasting
time arguing."

Wilde jumps in and waves me over. Fuck it, if we're
gonna get caught might as well do it together. We get
comfortable before the pile of sheets covers us. It's silent.
Wilde hasn't said a word, so all we can do is wait.

My thoughts go back to Jinx. Does she think of me at
all? Or has she forgotten about me? It's one reason why
I need to get back. I know I'm no good for her, but being
away isn't good for me. I can't do it.

The sound of a door rolling open has Wilde tense up next to me, a guy, and I assume the older woman's voices are muffled as they speak. The laundry basket jerks forward and knocks us into each other when we go over a bump.

"Fuck, this plan better work," Wilde whispers.

"It better. My life is in your hands."

We come to a halt, and another door slides closed. Another round of silence, and I'm not sure I'll be able to take it. If I wasn't claustrophobic before, I'm turning into one now, the sheets are weighing down on me, and I'm about to lose my shit.

Above our heads, three loud bangs echo through the air, causing both of us to flinch reflexively. Suddenly, the truck springs to life with a thunderous roar. Our freedom is coming to life; I can't believe Wilde's plan worked. We escaped that hell hole.

"You guys can come out now," the guy yells from the front.

We toss the sheets off, letting the daylight in. I peer around and notice we're chilling in the back of a cube van surrounded by even more laundry bins.

Wilde nudges me and grins. "Not so bad. Told you I could do it."

I kick the sheets off more, trying to get my entire body free. "Yeah, we'll see. I still need to get back to the school."

Wilde climbs to the front and shakes the dudes hand. And I'm left wondering what the hell is going down. I haul myself out of the bin and stand behind Wilde's seat. The guy driving isn't what I pictured at all. I think he's probably in his late thirties, with hair down to his shoulders, and seems to be completely covered in tattoos.

"Where am I dropping you two off?" he casually asks, as if he does this on a daily basis.

"I need to get back to Ravenwood Academy."

He looks over at me and grins. "A smarty pants, get out of here."

"I wouldn't go that far. Can you do that?"

"Yeah, I can drop you off at the gate on my way past."

I look at Wilde, and he shrugs. "I'll go where you go, Maddy."

Oh, if he only knew what he was signing up for. RWA doesn't treat people like us very nicely. This school chews you up and doesn't think twice about spitting you out. I can't blame the school for my fuck ups; I've been that way for years.

My nerves are on fire the closer we get to the school. I know for a fact that Ace is going to tear me a new one for leaving rehab, but he wouldn't understand. I wasn't feeling that place. But hey, gotta give myself credit; I made it five whole days. I know Jinx will be disappointed in me. I promised to get better, but I couldn't even do that. I'll forever be a failure; it's branded on my heart.

"This is your stop, fellas. Try to stay out of trouble." He stops the van just before the school gates, and I've never felt better in my life.

"Thanks again, man." Wilde gives him a pat on the shoulder before opening his door. "Oh, and you've never heard or seen us before." He jumps out and looks up at the gates.

I grab my bag and move in between the front seats. "Thanks, hopefully you don't get fired."

"Nah, I do this all the time. Keep your nose clean. Second chances don't come along all the time."

I think of his words as I climb out of the van. Is this my second chance? I've had so many I can't keep track, I can't keep doing this, that's all I know. I close my eyes and run my hand through my hair; this is going to be a mess once I cross that gate. I adjust my bag and head toward what could only be described as a torture chamber.

"Alright, Maddy. Give me the grand tour. Show me all the hot babes." He squeezes my shoulder and stares at the school.

"You're gonna hate it worse than Black Orchid."

He quirks a copper brow and rolls his eyes. "Maddy, nothing is worse than that place. The staff alone at BC are worse than the Devil himself."

Maybe I should've told him what happened or what is still happening here—death, stalker, and who knows what has been happening since I've been gone. I haven't been in contact with anyone, which makes me nervous. Being out of the loop doesn't help.

"You'll find out soon why this place is a shit show." As I pass through the steel gates adorned with the letters RWA, the school's heavy presence begins to engulf me.

The stone building is four stories tall, topped with a high peak roof resembling a cathedral. Two grand towers flank the main entrance, giving it a majestic look. The outbuildings are made of stone and have the same green roof as the main school. I have to say, it's a pretty nice sight to see. But my favorite building will always be Darrow Hall and that tower where Jinx lived.

We make our way down the road, and Wilde looks like a kid in a candy shop; his head can't swivel fast enough to watch all the chicks walk by. He nudges me when he sees Lula walking to Greywood Hall.

"You stay away from her if you want to be friends with my girl, I'm warning you now. That one there is off fucking limits."

"Why?"

"Because Lula has been sabotaging every chance Jinx gets into a better school, and Lula here loves to sleep with the music professor. Or did before I ran him off the road."

"Oh, really." He watches her step inside the hall. "I love a challenge. Let me have a go at her. She'll be singing a different tune."

"Wilde, I'm serious. Don't think about it."

He slumps his shoulders and exhales. "Fine. But it could've been fun."

As much as I would love to see Lula be knocked off her pedestal, I can't let Wilde get involved with anyone in this school. Stepping into Darrow Hall is like coming home. The fourth floor is where my heart truly lies. It feels like I've been away for much longer than just five days.

Every step seems like it's closer to doomsday. Something feels off, and I can't place my finger on it. Stopping at my door, I turn to Wilde.

"Something doesn't feel right."

"In what way?"

I can't quite put my finger on it, but there doesn't seem to be much happiness behind this door.

Fourteen

Ashton

I'm losing my mind. I've searched this entire school but can't find Jinx anywhere. It's been five days, and I'm thinking the worst. Did she leave us again? Did her stalker find her, and she's lying dead in the forest? I haven't talked to Atticus in days. I had to get away from his anger. If I had to listen to him bitch about Jinx leaving alone once more, I was gonna lose my shit. It also doesn't help that Archie was useless and couldn't help.

Spencer has been silent around us and actively avoiding us. It seems like he holds us responsible for Jinx's disappearance in some way. In a way, I can't blame him at all; we snatched his best friend away when we moved here. I get why he and Jinx were so close; we took her right from his side.

I send another text to Jinx, begging her to come back and I hope she's safe knowing it'll go unanswered. I don't want to give up because what if that message is the one she finally answers? I move around Maddox's dorm, waiting for my phone to ding.

I moved in here a couple of days ago when Atticus threw a glass at my head. I couldn't take it anymore. I've been leaving the window open, hoping Edgar would visit, but even he hasn't returned. My only reminder of her is her cello sitting in the corner and her clothes thrown across the bedroom floor. I need her back; my demons are slowly creeping back in, and I'm not strong enough to fight them off without her.

The dorm door flings open, and I swear if Atticus has come in here to bitch at me one more time, I'll knock his fucking teeth out.

I pinch the bridge of my nose and exhale. "Ace, I'm not in the mood." I turn around and freeze. I'm not sure if what I'm seeing is true or not. I check the date on my phone and look at Maddox. There is no way he can be here. He can't be here.

"Ash? What are you doing in here?" He walks into the room, trailed by a tall guy rocking a man bun and some serious piercings that would put Atticus' tattoos to shame. How can someone handle that many piercings on their face? The eyebrow, horizontal, eyebrow, bridge, snake bites, septum, and double nostril. I can't imagine trying to clean all of them.

I raise my brow at Maddox and his new friend. Maddox points to him, and I nod.

"This is Wilde. I met him in rehab." He says it so casually that I'm not sure how to act. It was five days.

I look down at my phone and pull up Atticus' name because hell if I'm doing this alone.

Me: Get to Maddox's room now. It's a fucking SOS!!!!!

"Why are you in my room? Where's Jinx?" He tosses his bag on the couch, and I watch Wilde walk around the room. I'm not sure how I feel about him. He has yet to say a word, and that irritates me.

"Can you sit the fuck down or something?" I finally snap at him.

"Oh, sorry. I've never seen inside a dorm room before. I find it interesting." He sinks on the couch, tapping his knee with his fingers.

"Ash, answer the questions."

I can't handle this alone; I'll crack under the pressure, and Maddox is fragile. I don't want to be the one to mess him up and have to take the blame for it. Once he finds out about Jinx, it's game over, and I'm not sure about this Wilde guy; what good is he to Mad?

"I need you to answer some questions first. Who is he?"

"Oh, that's Wilde."

"Yep, we established that, Mad. But who is he?"

They look at each other and shrug. "I'm Wilde, and I'm a recovering heroin addict. I was in Black Orchid for two months before Maddy came along. Let's skip all the bullshit, I helped him escape today so he can get back here."

"You fucking escaped, Maddox?" I'm at a loss for words. Who is this guy? Because the Maddox I know would never think about pulling a stunt like this.

Atticus bursts through the door, his hair disheveled and his shirt halfway tucked into his gray sweats. He gives the room a quick scan, and then he locks eyes with Maddox.

"The fuck is going on here?"

"We were just getting to that, brother." I cross my arms and wait for Maddox to explain why he escaped.

"It's not that big of a deal. Wilde knew I wanted out, so he helped me out. I'm here, and I'm sober. Can't we just move on? Where the fuck is Jinx?" His jaw twitches when he stops talking.

Atticus looks at me, and it's a look that says we need to tell him. If not, this will only get worse for us. But I don't want to be the one who has to break the news. You can call me a coward, but I can't do it.

"Does he have to be here? I don't know him." Atticus points to Wilde.

"He stays. Spill it."

Atticus shakes his head as he walks to the open window. "Five days ago, Jinx went missing."

Maddox jumps to his feet, almost toppling the coffee table over. "What?" he yells, waving his hands around. "And you didn't think I should've known sooner?"

"We determined it was best that you did your two weeks without worrying. We didn't want to jeopardize your progress. Sorry that we tried to look out for you."

"Don't give me that bullshit, Atticus. You've never looked out for anyone besides yourself. Should I ask what you did because this has you written all over it."

Atticus acts quickly, catching me off guard. Before I know it, his fist collides with Maddox's jaw, causing him to stumble backward onto the couch. Wilde and I rush to restrain Atticus before he can throw another punch.

"That's enough, Ace." I get in his face, trying to block his view of Maddox. "Don't, he didn't mean anything by it. Let him process what you told him."

Atticus pushes Wilde off him, and I dart a glance from him to Maddox. I'm glad he's here because Maddox also needs a friend, and I can't be in two places at once.

"That's no excuse for what he said. I might be an asshole, but I would never put Jinx in harm's way."

"I know that, and deep down, you know that. Jinx means everything to you. Now, can you act civil?"

He groans. "Yeah, but I swear I won't think twice. I'll beat him into the ground if he says something again."

I pat him on the back. "Good. Now." I turn to Maddox. "Smarten the fuck up, sober or not, that comment wasn't called for. You have no idea what we've been going through. Every day has been one huge torture test. There hasn't been a sign of her, not a note, nothing. We have no clue where she is. She vanished into thin air."

Maddox rubs his jaw, staring at the wall. "When was the last time you saw her?"

Atticus explains softly, "When we were at swim practice, she had to go to the restroom, and then she was gone," his voice trailing.

"And nothing since, no note, phone call?"

"No. It's been radio silence. If someone kidnapped Jinx, why haven't they reached out to us?

"May I ask something?" Wilde says, taking a seat next to Maddox.

I wave him to go ahead because what isn't there to be asked at this point.

"You checked every place in this school?"

"Yeah, every building, room and nothing." I tore almost every room apart, hoping to find a clue, but nothing. I came up empty every time.

"This school is older than dirt. There have to be secret doors somewhere that you haven't figured out yet. What about the basement? Does this dorm have a basement?"

"It's the laundry room. Trust me, I checked it. Nothing, not even a shoe left behind."

The only thing left is burning this entire school to the ground. Because if the asshole that took her, or if she doesn't reach out soon, I'm going to lose my shit.

"Have you gone to her dad's house?" Maddox asks.

Atticus looks at me. "Didn't think of that, to be honest. After what happened, I didn't think she would want to go back there."

"I didn't either. I'm not even sure if Mom still hangs around there."

This entire thing has my head in a mangled mess. Searching her dad's house never crossed my mind. What if she's been there the whole time? I only want her back and an explanation. I can't stop thinking that she didn't just walk away from us; something terrible happened instead. I'm beating myself up for not enabling her location. It's driving me crazy trying to figure out what happened.

"Where's my car keys?"

"Back in our room."

"Let's go. I'm not gonna be able to rest until we check that house." He stands and heads for the door. It doesn't feel real that Maddox is back or Jinx is gone. This can't be my life right now. My only concern is that Maddox is going to relapse since he didn't do the entire two weeks. And what happens if I'm not there to pick him up this time?

"Maddox, wait." I can't let him go. He can't be disappointed if she isn't there. "I think you and Wilde should stay. I don't want you to go in case Mom is there."

He pins me with his deep hazel eyes. "Ash, I don't give a shit about Serena. I'm headed there. Now, go get my fucking keys."

I'm done. I'm not starting a fight; I'm mentally exhausted, and trying to convince Maddox otherwise is like talking to a brick wall. From the look on Atticus's face, he feels the same way. I guess we're all taking one giant field trip to Grovedale.

Fifteen

Atticus

I feel like Maddox is even more stubborn than I am. And why is that Wilde dude tagging along? I just don't get it. What's his deal, anyway? I swear if he stares at me one more time, I'll tear his fucking lip ring out. I'm not sure he's a decent friend for Maddox; what person would help anyone escape rehab? Maddox needs to get clean. His mindset isn't made for this school, and now that Jinx isn't here to calm him, the whole thing is a mess.

I'm beyond pissed as we walk back to mine and Ash's dorm. Who is he to boss me around? Yes, it's his car, but his mental health is more important than being at that house and having a breakdown. But what the fuck do I know.

I leave all three behind to grab the car keys; for our sake, there better be something at the house. I grab the keys off the counter and my pack of smokes; I have a feeling I'll be smoking all of these today. The amount of stress is going to do me in. I toss the keys to Maddox, and he simply walks off without saying anything.

Wilde talks to Maddox like they've known each other for years and not days. I'm not sure how I feel about him yet. He has to have an angle; why did he want to leave the rehab before his time? Something isn't adding up. I step outside, grab a smoke, and light it up. As I take a deep drag, I feel the nicotine flowing into my lungs. Blowing the smoke out my nose, I feel calmer. Even if it won't last long, it's nice.

"I have a bad feeling about this," Ash leans in close and whispers to me as we stroll through the courtyard.

"Bad in what way?"

"This entire situation. Something feels off."

"You mean with Wilde or heading to the house?"

"With Wilde. Maddox doesn't usually make friends this fast; something is up, and I don't like it. Wilde hasn't let us in on his thoughts, but I'm curious why he's so focused on lending a hand and not bothered by the fact that we're all dating Jinx. That throws most people off, but not him."

I watch how Wilde walks—with his hand casually in his pocket and strutting like he owns the place; I can't help but want to knock that swagger right out of him. I need to figure out his angle and where the fuck he came from. No offense to Maddox, but no one wants to befriend him.

Once he starts talking about his parents, people usually begin leaving. It's nothing he does, and most people can't handle others' traumas. We had it easy with him; we saw firsthand what his parents were both like and knew we couldn't let him be alone.

Then, when Jinx came into the picture, she never thought twice about befriending Maddox either; it came naturally to her. Honestly, she tried to be friends with all of us, but I wouldn't have it. I still need to be her enemy in a way; I crave it—the fight she gives me fuels something within me. I need her back more than ever, and I'll never admit that out loud.

The ride into Grovedale is quiet. I don't want to talk with Wilde here. There are some things I want to discuss and having a stranger here for that isn't ideal. We need to ditch him and fast. For all I care, he can stay in Grovedale.

"What's so special about this house?" Wilde speaks, and I try my hardest not to punch the back of his head.

I shoot Ash a sideways glance, arching my eyebrow. He shakes his head, signaling it's not worth arguing about. But I beg to differ.

"Well, Wilde. " I plaster a fake smile on when he turns around. "If you knew anything about this family, you would know about the house. But it's only been five days. I wouldn't expect you to know anything."

"Atticus, seriously," Maddox scolds me. "Can't you be nice for once?"

"No. It might kill me, and I'm not risking that for a stranger."

Wilde holds his hand up. "It's fine, Maddy. People like him don't scare me."

As I see red, my fist tightens. "People like me. What does that mean?" Ash places his hand on my shoulder, keeping me firmly seated.

"It's not worth it. Let's just focus on finding Jinx and worry less about him."

"Fine." I grit my teeth. But I swear if he says something else, I'll lose it. He has no place to say anything about anything. I can't be holding things back forever. I'm about to burst with the amount of stress I'm under.

I try my hardest to keep my mouth shut when Wilde starts talking again. He doesn't seem to care that we are trying to find Jinx, and I don't know why that bothers me so much. He's like a stain that won't go away.

"We should come up with a backup plan just in case today doesn't go as we planned. We can't just sit around and hope Jinx shows up," Ash butts in.

Maddox gives me a look in the rearview mirror. I don't know what he's thinking, but I know he's still pissed at me for not telling him. I hope one day he realizes why I held it from him. As we pull onto the street we've seen a hundred times, I casually look out the window, trying not to think about the possibility that Jinx might be in that house. My heart speeds up a little at the thought.

I haven't been back here since Prescott's funeral; even if Jinx isn't here, this is going to hit hard. Maddox pulls into the driveway, and I can feel Ashton tense beside me.

"What's the plan? We all can't go storming in there."

"Ash is right. Wilde can stay in the car, Maddox take the back, Ash guard the front."

Maddox turns around. "And what about you?"

I pull the house key out and grin. "I'm gonna walk in through the front door, of course." I open the door, and the cool air hits me like a freight train. Something has to be in this house. I need a sign that Jinx is still alive.

As I carefully move towards the front door, Maddox heads towards the back. Ash follows me and positions himself at the front of the stairs. It dawns on me that maybe Ash should've gone with Maddox instead.

I've never been this nervous before; sticking the key in the lock, I take a deep breath and turn the key. The house is quiet when I step inside, can't tell if that's a good thing or not. I glance back and notice Ash keeping an eye on the front of the house. I make my way deeper into the house, and as much as I want to call out for her, I hold it back.

I move upstairs and check Ashton's old room, but nothing is out of sorts. I'm surprised Mom didn't pack everything and ship it to him or my shit, to be honest. I quickly make my way down the hall to the room that used to belong to Jinx. Unlatching her door, I get a sense of nostalgia.

I've been in this house for a week and still can't stand it. Odette has been getting on my nerves every second. Either she learns her place fast, or I'll teach her. She irritates me with the way she struts around this house like she's the queen of the castle. I can't wait to watch her fall. But Odette is too perfect for that, and I have yet to see her do anything wrong.

"Atticus, stop it. I don't know how many times I have to tell you this, but staring at her isn't going to do anything."

I advert my gaze to Ashton and narrow my eyes. "You know what, brother. One day, she will be so far over her head in trouble that she will need my help, and I'm not sure if I will save her."

He scoffs and rolls his eyes. "And when that day comes, and you rescue her, I'll stand back and remind you of this conversation. You'll do anything for her, admit it."

"Almost anything for her, I have to draw the line somewhere. I can't always be there for her."

I don't see where he thinks of this shit; just because he has a hard-on for her already doesn't mean I will. She will submit to me in other ways, and that's all I want from her.

That was the first night I snuck into her room and watched her sleep. When it was her room, now it's nothing like it. I close the door and make my way to Prescott's and Mom's old room. I've never been in this room before and am unsure what to expect. The house is so quiet; it's giving me the chills. I don't think I've ever felt this on edge before.

I take a deep breath and place my hand on the door-knob.

"Atticus, just open the fucking door."

Swinging my arm back, I land a hit on Maddox's jaw, my heart pounding loudly in my chest. I don't even hear him cry out in pain. Trying to catch my breath, I force my racing heart back down my throat as Ashton rushes up the stairs in a state of panic.

"What the hell is going on up here?" Ash looks between the both of us.

I point to Maddox, and Maddox points to me.

"Fuckin' children. Did you find anything?" Ashton pushes Maddox aside and stands next to the door.

"I was about to find that out; what the hell are you guys doing inside? You left everything exposed. And where the hell is Wilde?"

"He's downstairs."

I rub my face and try not to lose my shit. "We are trying to find clues, and you let a stranger in the house. Did you not think this over?"

I swat Ashton's hand aside and open the bedroom door. I no longer have time for this; we need to move faster with Wilde in the house. "Did you search downstairs before coming up here?"

They look at each other, and that's all the answer I need. Fuckin' dumbasses. "Get down there now and look around. Jesus Christ, you two are stupid."

I leave them behind, stepping into Prescott's bedroom, and shivers race down my back from the cold. The walls of the room are a deep navy color, and there's a beautiful four-poster bed made of dark mahogany wood right in the center; the white duvet doesn't look to have been touched in weeks. On each side of the bed, there are two identical nightstands. Prescott's is tidy and organized, while Mom's is packed with magazines, lotions, and jewelry. Nothing seems to be out of the ordinary.

The bathroom looks no different; all of Mom's things are scattered along her side of the sink. Except Prescott's side is cleared away. It almost makes me wonder if she moved Roan in here already. I wouldn't put it past her; she never waits for anything.

I'm starting to lose hope that we'll never find Jinx. I leave the bedroom defeated, a feeling I don't like. The fact that I can't find her doesn't sit well; at least when she left me three years ago, I knew where she was, but now. I feel useless, and that's something I can't get on board with. I find the guys in the kitchen talking amongst themselves.

Ashton looks up when he sees me enter, and he must tell by the look on my face that I didn't find anything. "We looked everywhere, even in the basement, but couldn't find anything. There's just nothing here."

"And you for sure checked everywhere in the school?" Maddox asks once more.

"Yes." Ash and I say together.

Wilde raises a brow, and I try to ignore him, but my hand twitches. "Fuckin' say what you want because clearly, you have something on your mind."

With a nonchalant shrug, he pushes me over the edge. I charge at Wilde, locking him in a headlock and delivering a punch to his gut. He gasps with a silent cry when I land another blow. Wilde whirled around, his fist struck with unexpected speed, crashing into the side of my face and making dots dance before my eyes.

"Hey, calm down." Ash quickly pulls me towards him and says, "Maddox, help me out here." I fight against Ash, trying to get to Wilde.

Wilde is still trying to catch his breath when Maddox pushes him backward. "Maybe it was a mistake for me to come back."

"Are you serious? You're choosing a stranger over your best friends?" I spit out. "You know what, never mind.

Don't bother coming back unless you take out the trash. I'm fuckin' done."

I walk out onto the back deck, leaving them all behind. I can only help someone so much, and if he rather choose that asshole, then so be it. I can't be here when his world crashes again. He went to rehab for a reason, not to run away from it.

I touch my fingers to where Wilde punched me and flitch; that's gonna leave a bruise. I should've punched him in the nose and broke it. As I rest my weight on the railing, I breathe in deeply, feeling the chill of the air with no relief in sight. I feel like there might be something we overlooked. Even though I wish I could take a day to recharge and reflect, I can't. I'm starting to feel stuck and discouraged because I'm running low on ideas and hope.

"You doin' alright?"

I don't bother to turn around; looking at Ashton right now will make me snap. "I think we should go, think Prescott's car is still in the garage?"

"Ah, yeah. Jinx didn't want it, so she left it."

"Good, let's go. I'm done here."

He stays quiet as I head back inside, and I don't spot Maddox or Wilde as I head towards the garage. Even if I did see them, I wouldn't acknowledge them. There's nothing more to be said. When I find Jinx, I hope Maddox has his shit figured out.

Sixteen

Jinx

I woke up five days ago not knowing where I was or with who. And now that I'm awake, I wish I was still sleeping. I should have just waited for one of the guys to accompany me to the basement. And that's saying something, considering how much I cherish my solo adventures away from them.

I've been trying to escape this bedroom all week, but it's been no luck. I hoped every time a meal was brought to me, a knife would accompany it, but I have been outsmarted. I'm not sure where I am at the moment. The window is covered in so much dirt on the outside that I can't even see through it properly. Even if I were to get out, where the fuck would I go?

I've never been so helpless in my entire life before, and I hate it. Is this what a damsel in distress feels like waiting for her prince to show up because if so, it sucks.

I roll off the shitty dirty mattress and head for the window. With a small tap, I go back to trying to crack the glass. That's my only clue, but then again, I could be in any old building. I try to break the glass chunk by chunk, but it's useless. The glass won't break, no matter what I try; I need that knife.

The sound of the wooden door slamming against the wall sends me leaping and twirling in surprise. My heart drops to my feet when he stands there, holding a plate of food.

"I'm not eating that until you give me some daylight."

He groans and walks in. I look past him to the door and wonder how fast I can make it.

"Don't. I will catch you before you reach the door," he tells me in his robotic voice. He has yet to change out of his hoodie and show me who he is. Then again, I shouldn't expect anything less from the person who has been stalking me for months.

He sets the plate on the mattress and takes a bite of the sandwich—our daily routine. He signals that the food is okay, then opens the water bottle and has a drink. It's gross, but we're both still kickin'. Still not risking it with the food, though. He places the cap back on and tosses the bottle on the mattress.

"Eat, or you'll grow weak."

"Who gives a shit. Is having sex with a dead body not your thing?"

He dismisses me with a wave, then heads back toward the door. I quickly grab the sandwich and hurl it at him, nailing him in the back of the head. His sudden stop and slow pivot causes my heart to skip a beat as he rushes across the room. With a forceful push, he shoves me onto the bed, settling himself on my stomach.

I wiggle beneath him, trying to get free. "Get off of me!" I try to slap him, but he grabs my hand, pinning it under his knee. After not eating all this time, I don't have much stamina left to fight for a long time, but that doesn't stop me from trying. I raise my other hand and try and hit him again.

"Do it, and you'll regret it."

Living with Atticus has shown me one thing: never shy away from a challenge. I curl my hand into a fist and deliver a punch to the side of his face. He grabs his face, and I try to buck him off; when that doesn't work, I try to punch him again. But he's expecting it and grips my wrist tight.

"Odette. I didn't want to hurt you, but you left me no other choice."

Yeah, I'm sure. I dig deep, finding power within me, slamming my forehead into his face. He tumbles backward, gripping his nose. Despite the searing pain pulsing through my head, I push through it as I rise to my feet. Feeling woozy and unsteady, my vision blurs as I struggle to stay upright. I push through the feeling of almost passing out and reach out for the door. Today is definitely not the day that I give up.

"You bitch."

I spin around and notice my stalker trying to get up. His hood has slipped off, but he's got a balaclava covering his face, so I still can't figure out who he is. He shoots me a menacing look with his bright green-eyes as I slowly back out the door.

"Fuck you, you piece of shit. Find me again, and I won't be as nice."

"Don't forget that I know your every move. Do you think I'm letting you go so easily? Think again. Your one boyfriend knows me personally; take that little information home with you if you can figure your way out."

I'm not sure what that means; who does he know? I want to stick around and ask, but I also want the fuck out of here. I have this feeling in my gut saying I should stick around, but my brain keeps urging me to flee. I'm not sure what to do.

My brain wins in the end. If he knows one of the guys, he'll eventually show his face; creeps like him don't stay quiet for long. I slam the door behind me and find myself in a dark hallway. Should I head left or right? I hear him shuffling behind the door, and that's all I need to make a decision. I veer to the left, fingers crossed that it's the right way.

When my head starts throbbing even harder from that blow, I find myself using my hand to feel my way along the wall. As I make my way towards the end of the hallway, I realize I've made a mistake. I close my eyes and exhale as I turn around, praying I can pass the room before he gets out. The exit can't be far past that room. I brush off the pain and start running. Getting caught again doesn't bother me; what's important is that I gave it a shot.

I pass the room I stayed in, taking in the cracked open door. He somehow left without me knowing. He's probably laughing at my mistake and waiting for me. I push my body further, trying not to fall over, when I find a stairwell—finally, a goddamn break. I look up, but when I can't spot him, adrenaline shoots through my body, and I rush up the stairs.

Turning the corner, I am suddenly struck in the chest, causing me to fall hard to the ground. The pain coursing through my chest is unbearable. I try to suck in an air full, but the pain burns.

"Thought I would let you get away from me, Odette?" He gently moves a stray strand of hair from my eye while I catch my breath.

"Fuck...you," I manage to say.

He tuts at me. "Don't be like that. Come, we'll call the boyfriend and give them a message." He grabs my arm and effortlessly tosses me over his shoulder, causing me to let out a groan as his shoulder presses against the tender spot on my chest.

The flooring is weathered hardwood, and it's got a few gaps here and there. Something that you would see in an old building. I still don't know where this would be located; nothing like this is around RWA. We enter another room; his footsteps echo the further we go. I try to look up, but the pain only grows worse; whatever he hit me with caused some damage.

He drops me onto a dusty brown couch and snaps his fingers when I go to move. I lay back down and wait for him to dig his phone out of his pocket.

"What's your plan? Call and brag that you have me?" I gently massage my chest as I struggle to speak through the anguish.

He doesn't look up from his phone as he shrugs. "Something like that. It's ringing." He puts the phone on speaker, and my heart skips a beat when it connects.

"Hello."

He points at me, waiting for me to speak. I wish I could, but hearing his voice brings tears to my eyes. I never expected it to affect me this way, but after five days without hearing it, I realized how much I missed it.

"Start talking before I hang up."

"Atticus," I quietly say.

"Jinx?" Panic rises in his voice. "Where are you?"

My creepy stalker takes the phone further away from me. "She won't be answering any more of your questions."

"You sonofabitch. You better tell me where she is, or I'll fucking kill you."

"Yeah, I don't believe you. You've never killed anyone in your life, Banks. Now, do me a favor, will you?"

Atticus has gone quiet. And when Atticus goes silent, it's not good. Whatever he's thinking won't play out for anyone involved.

"You better start talking."

He tilts his head when I start to sit up. "I think I might have hurt your girl when I hit her with a hunk of wood. I forget how much smaller she is than me."

"Don't you fucking touch her!" His scream pierces through the room, and I can feel the depth of his pain.

I try to stand, but creepy stalker snaps his finger at me, and I halt. "I need something from you in exchange for her."

"What?"

"Oh, I can't tell you over the phone; I think we can do this in person, don't you?"

I can sense a smile in his voice as he speaks, and I'm feeling unsure about the plan he's keeping under wraps.

It's making me a bit uneasy. It could be a trap, and the guys could walk right into it. I can't let that happen.

"Alright, fine, give me the details."

"I'll text you the directions. Can't risk Doll-face here escaping before you get here. You have one hour, tick-tock."

He hangs up, and his fingers fly across the screen. I have an hour to come up with a plan before everything goes to shit.

Seventeen

Maddox

I didn't bother sticking around after Wilde and Atticus got into a fight; there's no point if all he's gonna do is bitch about Wilde being here, and clearly I know when I'm not wanted. I should've stayed in rehab; things might have been better off. Then again, if I didn't fuck up in the first place, perhaps Jinx wouldn't be missing right now.

I just can't wrap my head around it; in just five days, the guys still haven't found any sign of her. I mean, how do you lose track of someone? Whoever took her had to have been planning this for a while. That's all that I can conclude. That's why we can't find her, he knew the route he would take.

I slam the front door to the car and sit there, squeezing the steering wheel. I'm trying to stay calm, but the more I think about everything, the more I need something to drink or swallow. It's becoming all too much for me to take. But I can't think about myself all the time. Jinx needs me, and that's what matters.

"You okay, man?" Wilde asks when he gets in the car.

"I'm not the one that got hit. How are you?"

He shrugs me off. "Meh, it won't be the last time I piss someone off. What's the plan now?"

I don't know, and that's the problem. I feel like I'm running away again. I stare at the house and wonder if we missed another clue inside. This entire thing sounds like a broken record. *No clues, where is she?* If something doesn't break soon, I'll break.

Atticus rushes out of the house, phone pressed to his ear, eyes wide as he scans the yard. Finally, his gaze meets mine through the windshield. Ashton follows, waving his hands at Atticus, but only ignores him. I slowly get out of the car and hear him tell whoever he's talking to about giving him the details.

"Ace, what the fuck was that all about?" Ash grabs his arm, spins him around, and confronts him face-to-face.

"He took her." His eyes focused intensely on Ashtons.

"Who did?" I ask, even though I have a feeling I already know who.

Atticus turns his head, and his blue eyes darken. "Her stalker."

As I imagined, not that this helps. We still don't have her. "What's the plan now?"

"We have to do what he says. He's sending over directions to where she is. We have an hour."

"An hour? Where the fuck is she?" His phone dings, and I swear my heart drops out of my body.

"I'm driving. Let's go."

I want to argue with him, but I bite my tongue. It's not the time; the only issue is Wilde. I can't leave him behind, but I feel like this isn't something he should be witnessing, either. I feel like I should keep him close because he did help me out, but Atticus does have a point; I don't know him that well. I don't want to seem harsh by cutting ties after his support. Plus, I'd feel awful if something went wrong and he relapsed.

I open Wilde's door, and as much as Atticus hates the guy, I think we need him. "Can you move to the back? We need to get moving."

"Yeah, of course. I'll do whatever. Unlike a certain someone I listen when talked to."

I move out of his way when he slips out of the car. "Thanks, man."

I climb in, and Atticus glares at me. "I can't ditch a friend; we might need him."

He shakes his head and slams it into reverse. He can be pissed off all he wants; this isn't about anyone in this car. The entire car is silent as Atticus drives. My mind wonders to what we potentially will be walking into. Jinx needs us, so no matter what, we have to be ready. I can only hope that nothing goes wrong.

We turn down a gravel road, and Ashton climbs over the seat, wedging himself between Atticus and me.

"Where the fuck are we?"

I lean forward, trying to figure that out.

"I know where we are," Wilde speaks up. "This is Whispering Lane. Where all those multi-million-dollar houses were supposed to be built."

"Supposed to? What happened?" Ashton asks.

"I heard the developer disappeared, some hotshot from the city. Most of these houses are undeveloped and left abandoned."

"What a joke; why not tear them down," I add. Who would leave these houses like this? Why not bring in another developer? All this land is going to waste.

Atticus makes another turn onto an unfamiliar road, and the overgrown trees line the way. I can feel my heart drop as a house comes into view. Its once-white paint is now chipping away, revealing the dull wood underneath. The windows are boarded up, and the front porch is nearly collapsing. Jinx is somewhere inside this massive house.

"What does he want exactly?" Ashton asks without taking his eyes off the house.

"He never said; he only told me he needed something."

That sounds ominous if you ask me. What the hell does he want? He already has Jinx, and he's been tormenting her for months. What now? I hesitate for a moment before taking a deep breath. The smell of decaying leaves fills my nostrils. I hop out of the car, the guys trailing behind me silently. The tall grass softly crunches beneath my feet as we approach the house.

Climbing the broken steps, we barely make it to the front door when it swings open, and there he stands, hoodie covering his face. My heart leaps into my throat as I take an instinctive step backward. Is it him after all this time?

"About time."

He's talking with one of those voice changers, so it's hard to tell who it is. He tilts his head, showing his dark green eyes and nothing more.

"You gave us an hour. We followed your instructions; what more did you expect?" Atticus retorted with an eye roll. Ashton elbows him and shakes his head.

His hand grips the door until his knuckles turn white. "For you to watch your mouth, considering I have your little girlfriend still."

Atticus moves forward, but I grab his shoulder to hold him back. "Don't," I whisper. "What do you want from us?" I turn to him and ask.

"A trade of some sort." He shrugs.

"What does that mean? You know what, never mind. Where's Jinx? I need to see her before I agree to anything else you have to say." Atticus steps closer and they are dang near the same height.

As Ashton moves in closer, crossing his arms, I join him, watching intently. Meanwhile, Wilde lingers behind, casually leaning against the damaged banister. Jinx's stalker doesn't move, cocky little asshole, I try to look past him, but he doesn't leave enough gap between him and the door. Jinx must be somewhere else in the house, or she would be screaming for us.

I'm so over this. I push past Ashton, slam my hand on the door, and give it a shove to open. Stalker asshole tumbles backward, falling to the floor.

"Try anything, and you won't find her."

Atticus grabs my arm, halting me from hitting him. "If I were you, I'd speak fast."

"Fine. You can have her, but I want him." He points to Ashton.

Ashton frowns and looks at him, confused. "What the fuck do you want me for? Who trades a human for another human?"

"That's not how this is gonna work." I grab him by the ankle and drag him over the uneven floor. The temptation to beat the crap out of him overwhelms me. My knuckles ache to connect with his jaw, to feel the satisfying crunch of bone.

In a moment of reckless abandon, I throw all caution to the wind and let my fist fly. Another satisfying crack of my knuckles meets his jaw, echoing through the room, a physical manifestation of my pent-up

frustration and resentment toward him. Despite the pain in my hand, I feel a sense of release and satisfaction.

He lay there for a moment, dazed and disoriented, before slowly pushing himself up. "You'll pay for that." he snarls, his eyes filled with rage.

I shrug, trying to appear nonchalant even though my heart is racing. "Do you think I give a shit? Now, where is Jinx?" I reply, my voice sounding surprisingly calm.

He lunges at me, but I'm faster, dodging his attack and striking him again, this time in the stomach. He doubles over in pain, wheezing for air, and I take the opportunity to kick him in the ribs. I can feel the bones cracking beneath my foot, but Wilde and Atticus pull me back before I can land another. But I want more. I crave more; I want him bleeding out on the floor.

"He can't tell us if you kill him," Atticus hisses.

I struggle to break free from their grasp. "I don't care." I grit my teeth when their fingers dig further into my skin. "Want him dead."

He rolls over, coughs, and groans. Serves him right—piece of shit.

"That's enough, Maddox," Wilde warns me.

"He better start talking, or he won't be walking again."

Ashton bends down next to him, slipping off his hoodie. He reaches for the black balaclava when a clash comes from a back room. No one moves or says anything. The prick starts laughing.

"That'll be doll trying to escape."

I go to move, but Atticus beats me to it, kicking him in the broken ribs. I can't help but feel a twinge of satisfaction as his screams echo through the room. Ashton goes for his mask again, and nothing gets in his way this time.

Ashton trips backward and gazes at the unmasked stalker. "How? Why?" he asks with horrified eyes.

I'm confused. How does Ashton know this asshole? I turn to Atticus, and he looks just as scared.

Eighteen

Jinx

I can hear the guys from the room that I'm locked in. No matter what I do, I can't get out. The chair I threw at the door was my only hope of getting someone's attention. And that apparently didn't work. I try to pry open the window once more, even though I know it won't budge. This place is damn near falling apart, but not enough to where I can escape.

Whatever is going on out there, I can only hope it's working in our favor because I can't stay here one more day. My chest throbs in pain when I try to push on the window more. I don't have much more energy left in me. I sink against the wall, slipping to the floor. I keep trying to take deep breaths, but it feels like I'm struggling more and more. I kinda have a handle on my asthma, but I'm starting to worry it might spiral out of control.

I close my eyes and concentrate on the noises beyond the room. But I can't hear shit. Whatever is happening must be occurring further away from me. I muster some energy and grab a piece of the broken chair; one way or another, I'm getting out of this room.

I forcefully slam the chair leg into the glass, causing it to shatter into pieces. The chilly breeze from outside stings my cheeks, but oddly, it feels refreshing. I run the wood along the window frame, freeing all the glass. I stand on my tiptoes, looking outside. It's a fair drop, but I think I can make it.

I look around the room for anything else to stand on, only I would ruin the chair. I grab the broken chair and am thankful only one leg broke off, but the other leg doesn't look the best. I position it under the window and then gingerly made my way up. The chair wobbles as I try to steady myself, and my heart jumps into my throat. I lift myself onto the ledge, trying to keep the weight off my chest. The drop looks higher now that I have the full effect. What's the worst that'll happen? A broken limb?

I get my foot up on the ledge and brace myself. Sending a prayer to Lucy, I close my eyes, getting ready to push myself forward. The sudden bang at the door startles me, causing me to release my hold unexpectedly. I scream as I fall forward out the window.

The ground rushes toward me in a blur when I jolt to a stop; my feet dangle in the air when I look up. Some dude with a man bun is holding onto my wrist.

"I take it your Jinx."

"Um, yeah."

"Figured, should I ask why you were jumping out the window?"

I hang here, feeling the weight of my body increase as my wrist screams in pain from the pressure of his grip. It feels as though the skin is being ripped off. "Wanna tell me who the fuck you are?" I grunt, trying to swing my other hand to the window ledge. For all I know, this could be my stalker.

"I'm Wilde." He hoists me up by my arm. I attempt to kick my feet against the side of the house, but he forcefully pulls me back through the window, slicing my stomach on a shard of glass. As I land on the floor, I shuffle backward and shoot him a fierce glare.

"I'm not going to hurt you. I know the guys."

"Is that like a nickname or something? Where do you know them?" I press my fingers on the bloody cut and pray this night doesn't get any worse.

"Is Jinx a nickname?" He rips a piece of his shirt and squats in front of me.

"It's a curse." I dig my fingers into the floor when he presses the piece of shirt into the cut.

His green eyes pierce into mine, and he flinches. "Sorry. Can you hold it, and we'll find the guys? I'm sure they'll be glad to see you."

"Same. But you still never answered me. Where do you know them from?" Wilde helps me up, and the room spins. "I need a minute." I close my eyes, trying to make the world stop spinning.

"When's the last time you ate anything?"

I shrug. "Five days ago. I think. I'm not touching anything from a stranger." He steers me toward the broken-down door. With each step, my stomach burns when the cut pulls apart.

"I don't blame you, I wouldn't touch anything that asshole made either. You good to walk?"

"I'm not a pussy."

He nods and guides me out into a hallway. For a house that's falling apart, it's still well-built. Wilde whistles loudly when we come into the living area. How many places am I going to see before I get to that front door?

Footsteps thunder above and around as they run through the house. Their voices call out to me, and it's felt so long since I last heard them. Ashton is the first to appear. His blond hair is all over the place, wearing dark ripped jeans and a mint hoodie with paint stains on the front. His icy blue eyes take me in from head to toe, stopping at my stomach on his second look. His head jerks to Wilde.

"It was an accident. She was falling out the window, man. It was either that or a broken neck."

"I'm fine, Ashton. No need for more blood."

"I'll be the judge of that Little Swan. You have no idea what it's been like that last five days."

I take a deep breath, trying to control the rage that flared up. "You're right. I have no idea what sort of torture you've been through. Tell me, please, what it must've been like, not locked up in a basement with no food or water, a shitty mattress to sleep on, wearing the same clothes, and wondering when or if you would be saved. Must've been hard on you."

He moves closer, gently placing his hand behind my neck and drawing me nearer. Then, he rests his forehead against mine. "I'm sorry. I didn't mean anything by it. I'm so sorry; I don't know what I would do if anything happened to you," he whispers.

"Odette," Atticus yells from across the room.

"Always cockblocked by the other half. I should've eaten him in the womb." Ash groans before backing away.

Atticus quickly comes to my side, wrapping me in a warm embrace and nuzzling his face against my neck. I can't help but release a soft sound of discomfort as he holds me closer.

"I thought I lost you." He speaks against my skin.

"You'll never lose me, Atticus."

He pulls away, looking into my eyes. "But I could've. Look at you; you're bleeding." He pulls my hand away, and I grit my teeth when he takes the cloth away.

"It's fine. It's only a flesh wound."

"Jinx?"

I look over and find Maddox standing there. His knees buckle, but he doesn't come any closer. I try to rush over to him, but Atticus holds me back. I try to squirm out of his grip, but his hand only digs further into my cut.

"Atticus, let go," I plead, trying hard to get out of his hold.

"No. Let him come to you. He needs time to process what's happening. Just give him a minute. He's been through a lot as well."

I'm more confused about how he is here. He should be in rehab. Maddox moves slowly toward me and places his hand on Atticus' shoulder.

"I'm good. I can handle it."

Atticus gently lets go of me and places his own over Maddox's, turning to face him as he speaks with compassion. "If it gets too much, walk away."

He nods, and Atticus walks away. What the fuck is going on?

"Jinx? What happened?"

I look at my stomach; the bleeding has stopped, but the blood on my clothes looks worse than it is. Even wearing a black shirt, it looks terrible. "Oh. He pulled me through the window, and a shard of glass cut me." I point to the guy named Wilde. The one I still don't know anything about.

Maddox snaps his head in Wilde's direction. "Listen, Maddy. I would never hurt your girl, and you know that. But she was ready to jump out the fucking window."

"The fuck Jinx." Ashton scolds me.

"Don't fucking start with me, it was either that or face the creepy stalker," I shot back.

Maddox places his hand next to my cut and pulls the cut shirt away. "Did the asshole touch you?"

"Him?" I point to Wilde again.

Maddox shakes his head. I kinda figured it wouldn't be him, but not knowing where *Unknown* is, I don't want to talk about him. Being in this house has my nerves on fire.

"Where is he? Have you seen him?"

Ashton and Atticus look at each other, and I know that look. They won't be saying shit to me anytime soon.

"I kicked the shit out of him. Don't worry, he won't be coming after you again, baby."

"I have so many questions but don't know where to begin."

"I think we should get you to the hospital and take care of this, and then we can talk." Maddox envelops me in his embrace, radiating warmth that instantly comforts me. I shut my eyes, breathing in his familiar scent that I've longed for. His absence has been hard to bear, and being in his arms again is like coming home.

"I've missed you, Maddox."

He rests his chin on top of my head and rubs my back. "Same, baby, same."

"We should get out of here and take care of everything," Wilde mutters to whoever is listening.

"He's right, and Jinx needs to get some rest and a doctor."

"I'm fine, Ash. I don't need a doc."

"No, the hospital, then we will go back to RWA. Don't argue with us," Atticus raises his voice.

I pull away from Maddox and turn to the other three. "I'm good. Can we leave, please?"

Atticus tilts his head toward the door, almost like he's dismissing us. Always the one that needs to be in control. Before I move, I need to ask the burning question.

"Where is he?"

Again, Ashton and Atticus avert their eyes to each other. Wilde scratches the back of his head and shrugs. I swing back to Maddox, and he avoids me also. I'm not in the mood for guy bullshit.

"Someone better start talking, or I'm not leaving."

Atticus chuckles. "You'll leave, trust me, Little Grim."

I am about to voice my thoughts when Maddox suddenly lifts me, gently holding me close in his arms. Despite my initial urge to protest and resist, a wave of exhaustion washes over me, making it impossible to do anything but surrender.

"All words, aren't ya." Maddox chuckles.

"I'll fight when I'm back to one hundred."

"And maybe that's when we'll tell you about *Unknown.*" He smiles at me like that'll make it all better.

I knew he knew something. Why they have to hide shit from me, I'll never understand. Even after everything I've been through, they can't tell me. I know they unmasked him, but what they did with him is what I need to know. Where is he?

"Don't worry, we'll tell you. He can't get you if you're worried about that." Ashton reassures me when Maddox walks next to him.

"That doesn't help me though. He tormented me for months, and you think that'll go away just because you said he can't get to me."

Ashton stops Maddox. "Maddox and Atticus kicked the shit out of him. So, trust me when I say this. He can't get to you."

I look over to Atticus, but he ignores us and steps outside. Maddox tightens his hold on me as we step outside. As the cool night air hits me, I can't help but feel relieved to be out of that place. I'll admit this exit is much better than going out the window, but I wanted to rescue myself. I wanted to prove to myself that I could do something on my own.

Maddox places me on my feet next to his car and tilts my chin up. "Are you sure you don't need the hospital? I'm worried about that cut getting infected."

"I'm fine. I don't know how many times I have to stress that to you."

He raises his hands. "Okay, I get it. Get the fuck in the car," he yells at the guys. "Get in the middle and rest."

I climb inside, and Atticus and Ashton sit on either side of me while Maddox climbs behind the wheel. The trunk slams shut, and Wilde climbs in front.

"We're ready," he says, brushing his hands off his jeans.

I go to look behind, but Atticus stops me. "It's not important. try to forget about this place."

I want to forget, but it's not that easy. I spent five days there, never knowing what creepy wanted from me. I don't think they'll ever know what it's like to try and get sleep when you never know if he'll walk through the door or if the meal you are supposed to eat is poisoned. It never made me feel any better just because he had a bite.

I watch the road zip by as Maddox drives; wherever we are, it's not well-traveled. I attempt to find some rest, but it just won't seem to happen. Even as Atticus gently places his hand on my neck and guides me into his supportive shoulder, his fingers soothingly stroking my head, the tension just won't release from my body.

I'm afraid it never will.

Nineteen

Ashton

I didn't think we would get her back after all that went down. I watch Jinx lean on Atticus. Despite her dark hair tangled in knots and dirt-smudged across her face, she remains undeniably beautiful. I can tell she's exhausted, but she refuses to sleep. I can't blame her; she's been through hell these last couple of days, and her body is in fight or flight still. We're lucky that she's letting us touch her. I can only hope it doesn't hit her out of nowhere when she doesn't expect it.

The drive seems longer this time around. I have questions for Jinx, but I'm afraid to ask them. Will she be open and answer them? I know for a fact that once she asks about *Unknown,* I'll break down and tell her everything, but I can't. I need to keep that information away from her until we all tell her together.

We pull into RWA, and Jinx sits upright and leans forward. "Nothing's changed."

"Same old rich dirtbags, baby."

"How's Spence? He must be losing his mind." She looks at me.

I run my hands through my hair, trying to think of how to answer that question without sounding like an asshole.

"He's been ignoring us," Atticus pipes up.

"Why?"

"Because he blames us and wouldn't listen when we tried to explain anything. He wants his best friend back, and we took her from him, not just now, but when we moved here. We haven't let you guys have any time together."

She faces the front without saying anything. "I'll call him."

I hate to break it to her, but she doesn't have a phone. That's one thing we never found at the house, and it's another burning question. Where the fuck did he take her from? Maddox drives around back, parking in his usual spot. He looks over at Wilde, and Wilde just nods. Then they both get out. I'm glad that Wilde is here because we wouldn't be able to handle Jinx and the asshole that's in the trunk. I open the door and hear a bunch of people yelling.

"I take it Cam is having another party?"

"When isn't he? We'll take the backway to the dorms, so no one sees you." I slide out of the car and spot a few dickheads in the parking lot watching us. Before Jinx gets out of the car, I slip off my hoodie and lean back in. "Put this on; I don't need anyone looking and spreading rumors about you."

Atticus exits the car and starts yelling at the assholes.

"He only makes things worse, you know that." She takes the hoodie and tries to slip it on but groans in pain when she raises her arms.

I grab it from her and pull it over her head. "I know this, but the dipshit doesn't get it and never will. Are you sure you're okay?" She works her arms into the sleeves.

"My chest hurts."

I lift the hoodie and her shirt carefully, and a dark purple bruise forms in the center of her chest. I gently touch it, and she grabs my wrist.

"Don't. He hit me with something hard, and everything hurts from it."

"Why didn't you say something earlier?" I gazed into her eyes, feeling her holding back her emotions from me. Yet, it's clear as day that she's going through intense pain.

"Because I can't afford to be broken. I need to be strong."

I pull her shirt down and cup her cheek. "Jinx. You don't need to be strong when you have all three of us. Scream, cry, or yell. Do what you need to; just let it out. We don't expect you to be perfect, and God knows we aren't, so don't you do the same."

She closes her eyes, leaning further into my palm. "I'm so tired. It was all my fault. He texted me, saying he knew where Dad's heart was, and I was stupid enough to believe him. I should've waited or told you."

"That isn't your fault. We would never blame you for wanting the remaining piece of your Dad. But believe me when I say this. He never had it and was only feeding on your grief. I think the only person that has it is the one that murdered him."

A sob lashes from her chest, and I tuck her into my body. Atticus pops his head into the car and gives me a fierce glance. I silently utter *Dad* to him, and he acknowledges me with a nod of understanding. I wrap Jinx into my arm and slide back out of the car. I nod at the guys to start walking; I'll let her cry for however long she needs to.

"Wilde is gonna hang back and take care of a few things for us. I told him he could crash at my place for the night."

"Good, we need to take care of something ourselves." Atticus looks over at Jinx.

We head down the path, trying to avoid the large crowds that are forming. Leave it to Cam to throw a party midweek. I swear he does it just to piss everyone off. Jinx buries her face into my chest when we walk past the noise.

"I'm glad we don't live in that house anymore; I would kill that SOB."

"I still wanna kill him, either way." Cam has it coming; our hit list is growing longer than we can keep up with.

"I can't believe he's back at the school after everything he pulled."

Jinx's fingers tense around my neck when Maddox says that. There's something she isn't telling us. There are so many secrets she's hiding, and it's time for Little Swan to come clean. She needs to understand that we are a team, and even though we get upset, we aren't upset with her. It's the situation, and we don't have control over it. Especially now, without Prescott around to help, things are getting harder for everyone.

"Either way, we'll take care of him. He can run his mouth all he wants, but it won't get him far," I tell Maddox.

Maddox scoffs. "Yeah, until his granddaddy says something. How do you think he got back in. The rich always find a way."

"Yeah, well. Not this time. It's time we take control of this school once and for all."

Something in Atticus' voice made Jinx crank her head to glance at him. Her eyelashes glistened with tears, and her cheeks were marked by their touch. She fixed her eyes on him, those eyes that seemed to see every thought and feeling.

"I have something to tell you about Cameron and that entire situation."

"Jesus Christ, Jinx. What don't you have to tell us." Maddox shakes his head.

"I wasn't raped."

We all come to a stop. The guys glance at me, and I inhale deeply, swallowing the lump that quickly formed. "That's good." That's all I can muster up to say; I didn't think it would still be a tricky subject to talk about. That prick wouldn't be breathing still if he did. Her fingers weave into my hair, pulling me out of my thoughts. I look down at her, and she smiles. I try to smile back, but I can't; the idea of him touching her turns my stomach.

Atticus comes up behind me, leaning his forehead on my head. "She's alright, brother."

"She's not."

Maddox approaches and gently takes Jinx away. And then Atticus gently embraces me, offering comfort and support. I'm forever grateful to have him as my brother. Jinx lovingly embraces me, and Maddox joins in, enveloping me in a sea of love, expressing their affection through their comforting presence.

"I'm not the one that needs all the attention."

"You are, Ash."

"Shut up and accept it."

"We'll always be here for you." Jinx hugs me tighter.

"Thanks. Can we get her back now?" I can't handle all this touchy-feely shit sometimes, especially when my emotions are heightened.

Maddox lifts Jinx back up, and we move along; the dorm comes into view, and a bunch of students roam around the entrance. The one time it's busy as fuck. Maddox hustles while Atticus and I run ahead and push our way through the group.

"Hey, watch it, asshole," someone says to Atticus.

He doesn't think twice; he turns around and punches him in the face. "You fuckin' watch it. You think you own this fuckin' spot?"

As his friend stands to swing, I quickly step in and deliver a punch to his stomach. He lets out a groan as he doubles over in pain. "I'd watch your back if I were you." I spit beside him. Everyone backs away when Maddox comes close, and Atticus opens the door.

"You don't own this spot either, you prick," the asshole says to Atticus.

Atticus turns and looks at everyone and laughs. "You'll see." He waits for me to enter before following.

"You guys can't fight everyone you come across. You know that, right?" Jinx scolds us as we walk up the stairs.

"We can, and we will, Little Grim. Don't make me beat your ass to prove my point."

She peers over Maddox's shoulder and raises a brow. If she weren't in pain, I would say Atticus would be testing out that theory on her. But I swear if he touches her until she's healed, I'll be beating the shit out of him.

We reach our dorm, and I punch in our code, letting everyone in. I feel so relaxed being back with everyone. If only we had time to relax; when Maddox places Jinx on the couch, she flinches from the pain. Atticus heads to the bathroom for the first-aid kit.

"Are you hungry? Thirsty? You know what, you don't have a choice." I move to the kitchen and look through the cupboards. We don't have much, but I guess it's better than nothing. I find a box of crackers and fill a glass of water.

I set the glass on the table and turn and almost drop the box of crackers. Jinx looks worse than she led on. The cut on her stomach looks red and enraged. That's a hospital trip, for sure.

"Jinx, what the fuck."

"I'm fine, Ashton. It looks worse than it is."

Maddox helps slip her shirt off, and I hear Atticus take a deep intake. The bruise looks worse than earlier.

"That doesn't look good. Are you sure he didn't break anything?"

"Yeah. It doesn't hurt when I breathe; it's just when I lift my arms, like when you do a heavy workout, I swear."

"And I swear if you are lying." Atticus starts.

"I'm not."

Maddox kneels next to her with the antibacterial and gauze. "Remind me again how Wilde did this to you?" He socks a piece of gauze with the antibac as she tells her story.

"I was locked in a room and broke the window with a broken chair. I was going to jump—" she hisses when Maddox starts dabbing the cut. He stops waiting for her to continue. "—jump out the window when Wilde came crashing into the room. That's when I got scared, slipped, and started falling, and he grabbed me. Needless to say, when he pulled me up, a shard of glass did this."

"So, he didn't do it on purpose?" Maddox confirms.

"No, he apologized but never did answer my questions."

He finishes up, and Atticus passes him new gauze and tape. "What questions?"

"Where the fuck did he come from?"

Maddox finishes, then stands, moving away from her. "He came from rehab. He helped me escape."

She tries to sit up but gives up. "Escape? What the fuck, Maddox. You were supposed to be in there for two weeks. Did they get a hold of you when I went missing? Is that why?"

"Don't blame them. I didn't know anything until I came back. That place wasn't for me. It wasn't right leaving you behind. I knew something was gonna happen. I shouldn't have left."

"You can't blame yourself, Mad," I tell him. I hate how he's always so hard on himself.

"You went there to get better, not to feel guilty," Atticus adds, squeezing his shoulder.

He shrugs Atticus off. "I know that, but it doesn't make me feel any better. I have a problem and will forever be struggling with it. You think a few weeks in rehab will magically heal me? I have to heal myself when I'm ready, and no offense, Jinx, this isn't helping me."

"Maddox, you do what you need to, but always come back to me."

"I can't do that to you again. What if I don't come back next time? I won't risk it."

"Then we take it one day at a time; it's been five, and we can do five more."

He falls to his knees, holding his face in his hands. Jinx casts a worried glance in my direction, conveying her desire to comfort him, yet unable to rise from her position. I move to Maddox's side, kneeling before him and embracing him.

He wraps his arms around my back. "I don't know if I can be strong, Ashton."

"You can. We all believe in you. You've been doing such a good job, and you have no idea how proud we are. Don't ever give up."

"I shouldn't be so worried about me when she's been through hell."

"It's okay to be selfish sometimes. You can't take care of others unless you are taken care of." I pull away, looking him in the face. "Are you gonna be okay?"

"Yeah, eventually, maybe."

"That's all I ask for. Now let's get some rest, and tomorrow we'll drill the shit out of Jinx."

I look back at Jinx and see that she has already fallen asleep. It's a relief to see her resting. I only hope her sleep is a peaceful one.

Twenty

Atticus

I quietly leave the dorm at the crack of dawn and head downstairs; I've never needed a smoke more than I do now. Having Jinx back should relieve me, but I don't feel any of that. The real shit is about to hit the fan, and I don't think any of us are ready for that. I know we should let the cops handle Prescott's murder, but they haven't done shit to figure that out. It makes me wonder if they are being paid off. I need to talk to Mother.

I casually grab my pack of smokes from my back pocket, take one out, and start to bring it to my lips. Just as I'm about to light up, I hear someone clear their throat from behind me.

"The entire dorm better be on fire if you are interrupting me."

"Did you find her?"

Spencer. Fuck. I like to light up my smoke, take a breath in the smoky goodness, then casually exhale as I turn around. "Yeah, we did."

"And no one bothered to tell me? What the fuck." He pushes his glasses up, revealing his sad grey eyes.

My heart goes out to him. While we felt some relief after locating her, he must have been constantly checking his phone, hoping for Jinx's call.

"Sorry, man, we didn't get back until late, and we had to patch Jinx up. She's inside my dorm, so if you need to visit, she doesn't have her phone."

"Yeah, thanks."

He doesn't move, and when I look at him again, I can tell something else is bothering him. I can't believe I'm feeling sorry for a dude who's been hanging around my girlfriend all the time. I must be insane to let another guy in our circle.

I try not to sound dismissive when I ask him. "What's wrong?"

He looks in the distance and sighs. "I should've been there for her, but I let her down. What kind of friend does that make me?" He turns and looks at me.

I chuckle at that. "What kind of boyfriend does that make all three of us? We weren't there either. Trust me, we all failed her. That's why we need to be there for her now."

"Did you find her stalker?"

I nod, taking another drag of my smoke.

"Who is he?"

I shake my head. "I can't tell you."

"Why? I think I have a right to know."

"Listen, Spencer. As much as I want to say, I can't."

"Can't or won't?" he scoffs.

I flick my butt on the sidewalk and head for the door. "Can't. I'm sorry. Are you coming up or not?"

"Yeah, I'll be up shortly."

Once Jinx finds out who her stalker is, I'm afraid she'll never recover. I'm having a hard time not going and beating the shit out of him again. I hope Wilde did his part and locked that asshole up good and tight because if he gets free before we can get to him again, I won't stop until I catch him.

I push open the door to the dorm and find Jinx standing by the window. I walk over and carefully wrap my arms around her stomach.

"Watcha looking for?" She leans into me, and her entire body relaxes.

"Edgar. Have you seen him?" she whispers.

Now that she's mentioned him, I haven't seen him in a while. "No. But I'm sure he's still around."

"I hope so; maybe he's been trying to get back to my old room."

She hasn't been back in her room since that bloody bird incident. But now that we have her stalker, I suppose she could move back, even though I'm not thrilled about it. I prefer having her nearby. Does that make me a clingy guy? Fuck I hope not, that's the last thing I need.

"Are you feeling better? We can take a quick trip up there if you want."

"Could we? I would feel better knowing he isn't trying to get in."

I place a kiss on her temple and move my hand to her shoulder, turning her toward the door. "Let's go before anyone wakes up." I look over at Maddox, who's snoring away on the couch. I'm glad he's getting the rest, but I'm also worried he's gonna slip up.

Jinx doesn't speak as we walk up the flight of stairs. I have no idea when we're gonna tell her about *Unknown*, but we need to tell her soon. We have to. And I hope Edgar makes an appearance soon; she needs that little bit of comfort that we can't give her. I hold the door open for her, and when she doesn't move, I place my hand on the small of her back.

"Everything okay?"

"Yeah. It's just the last time I was here; I thought Edgar was dead."

"If you aren't ready, it's okay. Some things take time; there isn't any pressure. We can always go outside and see if he comes to you."

She shakes her head. "No. I need this." She steps into her dorm and lets out a deep sigh. "It feels like years since I've been here, but it's only been weeks."

As we stroll deeper into the room, I can't help but notice how much of her presence remains here. The sweet scent of coconut still hangs in the air, a pair of fishnet stockings are casually draped over the couch, and a stack of cello books are neatly arranged on the coffee table.

I watch as she swipes a finger along her books. "I miss my cello. I'll never get into a symphony now. I've blown everything that I've worked for."

"No, Odette, you never did. I think this school was never meant for you. You should've gone someplace in New York, not here."

"I couldn't leave Dad." She pauses, then laughs. "Guess he left me instead."

"He didn't leave you, Jinx. He's still around. He raised you to be just like him."

She rests her hands on her hips, and just because she looks like her Mom, this is all Prescott. God, I miss that asshole. I walk over to the window and open it, needing a distraction.

"How do you call this little fucker?"

"He isn't a fucker, you asshole. And I've never had to call him. He always just...came."

We stand by the window, looking out to the trees, waiting for a blackbird to make its appearance. I'm not sure what to tell Jinx if he doesn't show. Her heart can't take much more that I know, but she might have to come to terms with the fact that Edgar isn't coming back.

"I don't think he's coming." She closes the window. "I'm headed back and gonna take a shower. I should've taken one last night but passed out instead."

"Sleep was more important than a shower, but you do kinda stink."

She shoves me and laughs. "Shut it. You wear the same shit for five days, and you tell me if you stink or not."

"I am a guy, we stink on a daily."

"Yeah, but you smell in a good way. I smell like sweat and." She pulls her shirt away from her face and sniffs. "Dear lord, I don't know what that is."

"Come on, let's get your ripe ass in some water."

"Watch it, Banks. Or I'll drown your ass instead."

"Your mouth is going to cause trouble for you, and if you weren't hurt, I would put you in your place."

Her pupils dilate, and she licks her lower lip. I run my thumb along her lip before tugging at it. "You get nothing until you're healed."

"I blame Wilde for cockblocking me."

I wrap her in a hug because that prick cockblocked me too. "Don't worry, you'll be healed in no time, and then I'll fuck your brains out."

"Can Maddox and Ashton join?"

"I'm sure they would beat me if they couldn't, but you know Ashton won't want anything from you."

We step into the hall, and she looks up at me. "I'll never pressure him, you know that, right?"

"I do. Ash won't do anything he's not ready for. But I'm afraid he'll never be ready."

"He will. It'll happen at his own pace. And no one knows when that'll be. Only he does. All we can do is be there for him and let him know that we support him no matter what he chooses to do. I'll be okay never having him in that way; all that matters to me is having him in my life."

I knew she cared for Ashton, but I didn't know how much. I should've known it ran deep. I shouldn't even say care; she loves him. It's clear how much she'll do anything for him, and the same goes for Maddox. I'm not sure about me, though. I think she hates me some days, which I don't blame her, I've been an asshole to her since I've known her, but it's been fun.

I barely open my dorm door and hear Maddox and Ashton having an all-out war.

"This will be fun. You have a shower; I'll deal with them."

"You sure?"

"Yes, whatever caused it shouldn't involve you. Go get cleaned up, and I'll get you some breakfast, and then we'll talk." I quickly kiss her on the lips, and she rushes off to the bathroom. I turn to the guys and whistle, grabbing their attention.

"What the fuck," I say slowly.

Ashton points at Maddox. "This asshole was drinking."

"It wasn't a drink, calm the fuck down."

Ashton digs a bottle out of the trash and slams it on the counter. "Then explain this."

I grab the bottle and read the label. "It has alcohol in it, so explain, Maddox."

"I was dumping it down the drain. I didn't want anything around in case I had the urge to drink. Is that okay with you?"

I want to believe him, and as his friend, I should be giving him the benefit of the doubt, but with everything going on, I wouldn't blame him if he did have a drink.

"Is that all the alcohol?" I nod to Ash.

"Yeah, we didn't have much here."

"Okay, good. Maddox, you good?"

He nods and moves back to the couch. "Yeah, whatever. No matter what I do, you guys won't believe me, so what's the point."

"It's not that, man. You've only been sober for less than a week. Can you blame me?" Ash walks behind the couch, leaning over. "I didn't mean to say that you're a shitty person by touching the stuff, but I only want the best for you."

"I get that, but just because there's liquor around doesn't mean I'm gonna have the urge to slam the shit back. Give me some goddamn credit."

"We are."

"The fuck you are, Ace. Ever since you discovered it was your asshole dad stalking Jinx, you think you can control everything. You can't."

"What?"

I swing around and find Jinx standing in the living room.

Twenty-One

Maddox

Me and my big mouth. This wasn't how I wanted Jinx to find out. I feel like an ass as I watch her standing there, her hair dripping water onto the floor, a towel haphazardly wrapped around her body, and a small pool of water starting to form around her feet.

She looks between Ash and Ace. "That asshole that has been stalking me for months has been your dad this entire time?"

"Trust me, I was shocked too," Ashton tells her.

"Where is he?"

Atticus turns to me. "We had Wilde take care of him."

"I don't understand any of this. Why did he do it?" She pulls her towel closer to her body.

"Come sit, please. We don't have answers for you."

She shakes her head and backs away. "He said he had Dad's heart; how would he know that? He showed me a box."

Ashton moves closer but stops inches away from her when she backs away more. "I don't know, Jinx. I'm just as confused as you. I haven't seen that prick since I was a kid. Mom made sure that he never came around. That's why I don't understand him coming around now and going after you. He shouldn't even know who you are."

"The things he said and did."

"I know, and trust me, he'll pay for what he did. You have my word. Wilde has him locked up, and he can't escape. I need some answers from him also." Atticus stands next to his brother.

"You don't think he killed my dad, do you?" she asked. A tremor shook her lips as she whipped a tear away.

The room grows deathly quiet. I never thought of that; my suspicions have always been with Serena or Roan, and I'll always believe that. But now that she mentioned it, it does seem odd that he would know where her Dad's heart would be, and why would he know that? Not the fact that someone would take an organ out of a human. That's a question for a different day.

"Jinx, I swear we had nothing to do with the death of your dad." I try to reassure her, but I don't even know if it's enough.

"Can I have a few minutes to myself?"

"You never have to ask," Ashton tells her.

She gives a little nod, then spins around and heads back into the bedroom. I move away from the couch to where the guys are standing.

"We need to call Wilde and figure this shit out now. Wherever he has your dad, we need to get over there now and have a chat with the prick."

"No shit. Nothing makes any sense anymore, and I don't like it. Why, after all these years, come after us, and why choose Jinx? I need some answers before I lose my goddamn mind." Ashton walks into the kitchen, opening a cupboard door only to slam it shut.

"We could call Mother and ask her."

Ashton swings around, glaring at Atticus. "Are you fucking stupid? That's asking for a can of worms to be opened. She'll want to know everything, and it's none of her fucking business."

"I would have to agree with Ash. Serena doesn't need to know shit, and to be honest, what if she's in on all of this?"

"If Mom were in on this, I would be amazed she could devise such a plan. And why, after all these years, would she talk to the sperm donor? What would she get out of it? She was married to one hell of a guy."

Atticus rolls his eyes. "She's a fucking idiot, so who the fuck knows what she's been planning this entire time."

I pull my phone out and send a text to Wilde, telling him we need to have a chat with the cunt. He sends back a message right away telling us where he's at. I laugh at the location, considering Wilde doesn't know this school.

"What?" Atticus asks.

"Wilde has your dad locked up in the old administration building."

"How the fuck did he find that place?"

I don't put anything past Wilde, but seeing how he got both of us out of that rehab without being caught still amazes me. It makes me wonder what Wilde did while he was out of rehab. I shrug at the guys because I can't answer that question. Even I haven't been to the old administration building, so who the fuck knows how he found it.

"Can we go somewhere?" Jinx asks when she emerges from the bedroom. She's rockin' black leggings and a hoodie, with her hair thrown up in a messy bun. Her beauty shines no matter what she wears.

"Where did you need to go?"

"The school basement. That's where I was taken from."

"Are you kidding me? We checked the basement; it's nothing but the laundry." Atticus runs his hand through his blond hair, frowning.

"Atticus is right. Is there another basement that we didn't know about? Ashton asks, looking lost. "I heard stories of a cult and would've been worried if they did laundry as a task."

I look at them like they are idiots. "Why wouldn't this school have a basement? It's old as dirt."

"Don't fucking start. We were going out of our minds trying to find her; you wouldn't understand." Atticus steps closer to me, poking me in the chest.

Another reminder that I wasn't here. I'll never live that down.

"Okay, boys, that's enough. The basement isn't accessible anyway, so I don't blame you for not trying. Either way, you did find me, and I'm safe. But please, can we go? I need to see something."

"Are you sure you're feeling better?" Ash taps his stomach.

"I'm good. I swear."

For some reason, I don't believe her. She hides her pain too well, so she doesn't burden us, especially when she knows if I've been struggling more than usual. I'm trying my hardest not to fall into the deep end, but knowing what I know, it's a real battle not to go out and grab a drink.

"Alright, let's go. I ran into Spencer earlier; I'm sure he'll want to stop by later since he never came." Atticus said, looking at Jinx.

"Can I use your phone? I'll text him."

Atticus digs his phone out and hands it to her. "Was he upset when you talked to him?"

"Would you be if your best friend was kidnapped and you weren't there for them?"

"You don't have to be a dick about it, I was only asking." Her fingers fly across the screen of the phone.

"I'm not being a dick, but if he's your best friend, maybe have some compassion for the guy."

Her head snaps up, and Ashton runs over and wraps his arms around her before she can say anything else. "Okay, that's enough. Emotions are still running high, and before you both say something you can't take back, we should go."

"I wouldn't regret the words that left my mouth."

"Jinx, that's enough," Ashton growls.

I head for the door before I get in the middle of that bullshit. It's bad enough that I let shit slip; I won't say anything about Jinx and Spencer. I step into the hall, and Wilde is leaning against my door down the hall. When he sees me, he pushes off and heads toward me.

"What's the plan?"

"Jinx wants to head to the school basement. You tagging along?"

He shrugs. "Might as well, I have nothing else to do."

"What are your plans now that you're out?"

"Maddy, I don't plan shit. I'll go wherever I can and pray that I survive another day. That's all I can hope for."

"I hear ya on that. You can stay in my dorm for as long as you need."

He raises a brow. "Won't the dean have something to say about that?"

"Don't worry about him. I have connections, and it's about time I started cashing in on them. And this fucking school owes me."

"Maddox Van Daren, are you using me now?"

I turn around and see Jinx standing there with a smile on her face.

"No, baby, never." I pull her into my chest and lean my lips to her ear. "But anytime I can, I will," I whisper. I lower my hand to her ass and squeeze it.

"You better watch it, or we won't make it very far."

"Heal first, sex later."

"You two are unreal." Ashton grabs Jinx and hauls her down the hallway.

I can't help but laugh. We all want to be with Jinx, but our patience isn't there. It doesn't feel like she's been back for one day, but I need to remind myself of that. Just because she's handsy doesn't mean she's ready mentally. I can only hope that her spirit isn't broken by this.

As we leave the dorm, we trail behind Jinx through the courtyard, attracting quite a few curious looks from passersby. I mean, it's not exactly common to see a bunch of dudes walking behind a girl without causing a scene. When you have a guy like Cam walking around, you're somewhat used to seeing it. We walk up the stairs, and Jinx pauses.

"Maybe I can't do this."

Atticus places his hand over hers and reaches for the door. "You can. You have all of us behind you. Nothing will happen. I promise." Together, they open the main door and step inside.

"How fancy is this school?" Wilde asks when he notices the checkered flooring.

"Fuckin' fancy," Ashton says. "Be prepared for a bunch of snobs, and don't start a fight because we can't get you out of anything."

"What he said." I wait until everyone is inside before turning around. Like, I figured someone was watching us. Cam watches with Liam, Shane, and Emery at his side. Whatever they have planned, I don't like it.

I feel like it's been forever since I set foot in this school. I'm still pissed with the entire Von situation; nothing has been resolved with that yet, and with my luck, he'll still press charges. I can only hope that he pulls his head out of his ass soon. Jinx takes us down a set of stairs, past a few offices. I've never been down before, and when she stops at a dark wooden door, she goes pale.

"He isn't down here for sure?" She turns and looks at Wilde, a line of worry materializing between her eyebrows.

"I swear he's still in the old administration building."

She goes to the door and pulls the handle. The door lets out a loud squeak as it swings open, sending a blast of chilly air toward us. I stare into complete darkness and find it hard to believe she did this alone the first time. Atticus turns his flashlight on his phone and shines it down a set of stairs.

"Where the fuck did he take you?"

"To hell, Mad."

Twenty-Two

Jinx

I didn't think I would come back to this God-awful basement. But after seeing that box, I need to know Dad's heart is there. I need to know if that box is still down here. I need to solve who killed him. The cops aren't doing their job, and that's another thing I need to do since being back. I would let it go, but I can't; I'll never be able to.

The further we walk, the harder it gets for me to breathe. I reach my hand out, needing some support. Because if not, I won't make it. My hand lands on a chest, and I fist their shirt.

"Hey, if you can't do it, don't," Atticus' voice cuts in.

I pat my chest, and I hear them all swear. I don't have my inhaler; I didn't think about grabbing my spare from the dorm before coming. Ashton comes into view; he takes my face in his hands.

"Breathe, slowly inhale."

I take a deep inhale.

"Good, now exhale."

I close my eyes and breathe out.

"Perfect, now repeat that."

I focus on breathing and his touch. I don't want to think about what's to come. I know *Unknown* isn't waiting for me this time, and I have all these guys with me in case something happens. Whoever shirt I'm still holding, they place their hand over mine, and I know from their touch that it's Maddox. I don't think I'm able to move forward without having another asthma attack. I point down the hall.

"The door on the right, can someone check it out for me? I can't."

"Of course." Ashton lets go and turns to walk when he stops and takes his phone out.

His flashlight lights up the hall. His light moves side to side the further he moves away from us; when it swings to the right, I can feel my heart race. When he walks into the room, my breathing picks up.

"Jinx, you need to breathe. Everything will be alright."

But Atticus is wrong; everything isn't going to be alright. Nothing will ever be okay. They don't understand what it was like being in that room. It was only the start of my torture, and I didn't know it then. I thought it would be the way to some answers, but I didn't get a single one. The thing that keeps racing through my mind is that nothing was in the box. The entire thing was a trap; I was the stupid fly attracted to honey.

"Jinx, Ashton can handle it. No one is in that room."

"Yes, I know that," I snap, pulling away from Maddox and moving away from the guys. I rest my head against the cool brick wall, trying to calm myself down.

"There's nothing in there. Except for your bag. Guess he wasn't worried about that being found." I can hear Ashton's voice echoing through the hallway. I don't know why I was expecting more to be found, but why leave my bag behind? Not that I'll be complaining about that. But I wanted that box.

I look toward the flashlight's glow, waiting for Ashton to lower it. "There wasn't anything else?"

"Sorry, Jinx. There was nothing." Ashton keeps the light close to the ground, and the glow lights up the entire area, but I can see the disappointment on his face.

"Can I see him?"

"No," Atticus said, steel in his voice.

I swing around and shove Atticus. "You don't get to tell me what I can or can't do." He grabs my arm and pulls me close.

"I can and will. You have no idea what you are asking. I know you need this, but I can't let you do it."

"Let me do it." I turn to Ashton, but Atticus pulls me back.

"Don't. He'll even agree with me. And don't bother asking Maddox. He has no clue what that prick is like. He fucking stalked you to get closer to Ash and me. You think I'll let you near him again?"

"I need to know where that box is."

"Then I'll ask him, but you aren't doing it."

I turn to Maddox and see Wilde looking out of sorts. He raises his brows and tilts his head toward the exit. I swear if Wilde is my white knight right now, I will lose it on the guys. I snuck away once; I don't think I'll be able to do it again. I slowly back away from Atticus and move to the other end of the hall where Wilde is.

"You can show me?"

"Um, yeah, I can."

"The fuck he can!" Atticus yells.

I don't bother turning around. I keep my eyes focused on Wilde. "Take me now."

"Jinx, I don't think that's a good idea," Maddox cuts in.

"I need this. You wouldn't understand."

"I do. If you think I don't, you're wrong," Ashton mutters.

My heart breaks, of course Ashton would know. After everything he went through, he still faced his enemy while trying to keep himself afloat. But he needs to let me do this; I don't care if it's his dad or not, and even so, you would think he would want some answers.

"I'm not arguing with you two; I'm going. You can join or not, but Wilde is taking me."

"I—Um. Shit, man, don't put me in the middle of your matrimonial spat."

"It's not a fight. She isn't going, and that's the end of this conversation." Atticus brushes past me without another word.

I chase after him, giving him a shove from behind. "You don't get to tell me what to do, for fuck's sake."

He pivots, grabs me by the throat, and slams me against the wall. "I suggest you start listening to what I fucking say, Odette. You don't know the guy, so stop pushing."

I push against his hand, feeling the pressure. "Or what?"

Ashton cuts the flashlight off, leaving us in the dark. Atticus pushes me back against the wall, and I feel his other hand on my hip.

His breath is hot on my neck when he leans in, his lips brushing on my skin in a teasing caress. "Do you want to know *or what*, Little Grim?" he whispers, his voice a low, gravelly growl.

"You can try it."

Atticus chuckles, his fingers trail along the edge of my waistband, making me shiver. "You know I always get what I want, Jinx." Sliding down my pants, his fingers slide between my lips, dipping into my wetness. I suck in an air full when he moves to clit and presses firmly. "Fuck, Little Grim. You're so wet already. Does the thought of having everyone listen to you turn you on?"

"Fuck, Atticus."

He slides two fingers deep inside while his thumb still rubs my clit; my knees threaten to give out the more he fucked me with his fingers; his hand around my throat tightens, and I can feel my inner muscles clamp around his fingers.

"That's right, come for me," he demands, his voice thick with desire.

My body shakes with force as I find my release, my moans echoing in the hallway, but he didn't stop his fingers from continuing their relentless assault. I grit my teeth as he continues his torture.

"You fucking listen to me and listen good. There will be no visiting that prick until I say so, do you understand."

"You asshole." I try and shove him away, but his hold around my neck is too much.

"That's right, and you best remember that." He takes his wet fingers and forces them inside my mouth; when he pulls them out, he slams his mouth on mine.

I move my face away and see three shadowy figures standing there watching. "Fuck." Wilde isn't someone I wanted to be watching or listening as I came.

"Yeah, you didn't think of our newest addition, did you?"

"Fuck off, you decided to stick your fingers inside of me."

He pinches my jaw, forcing me to look at him. "And I'll do it again, learn your place, Jinx. Now let's go."

He releases me, and I storm toward the stairs, not caring that I can't see. I can't believe him; if he had it his way, he'd never let me see *Unknown.* Well, two can play that game. If he thinks I'm going to bring him when I talk to his fucking mother, he can forget about it. That bitch wants to sue me for the school, anyway; it's not like it'll be hard to get her to see me. She'll crawl to me once I mention her getting the school.

The flashlight's glow lights up the view, but I don't stop. All of them can fuck off. I storm up the stairs. I can hear them chatting to each other, but I can't make out about what. Wilde said he's keeping *Unknown* in the old administration building. That's my new target when everyone goes to sleep tonight. Either way, I'm getting some answers; Atticus doesn't rule my life like he thinks he does.

When I make it out of the basement, I keep walking, not caring if they are pissed with me for not waiting. I need to make one pit stop before I leave the school; I missed so much, and I'm afraid of what all the professors have said to Allan. Florence will know what has been said.

"Jinx, you can't always walk away because you don't get your way."

"The fuck I can't, Ashton," I call over my shoulder.

"My God, woman, you are stubborn."

"And you aren't, Maddox."

I step into the office, and Florence looks up from her computer and looks at me in shock.

"My God, dear. I was worried about you. Atticus informed me about your stalker. Where have you been?"

"You don't wanna know. What did I miss?"

She waves me off, rolls her eyes, and points to the back offices. "Just Allan, pretending like he knows what he's doing. I swear he's been lost since you vanished. Roan has been sniffing around, and so has Archer. Those two are up to something."

"Great. Where's Allan now?"

"In his office. Did you want a meeting with him?"

"Maybe in a couple of days, I need to decompress first. If he isn't falling apart at the seams yet, he's fine. If Serena comes back, call me."

She nods. "Will do." She points at Wilde. "Who's this?"

I look over my shoulder at Wilde, then Maddox, looking for help. I didn't expect him to follow us into the office.

"He's a friend; he came to check out the place 'cause he was considering enrolling," Maddox tells Florence.

"Delightful. If you need anything, let me know. Ravenwood would love to have you."

I give Florence a wave, then push past Atticus. I don't get far when he grabs me. "Don't be stupid. I already know what you're planning, and it's not gonna work. I already told Wilde to move him so you can't run off and talk to him."

I rip my arm from his hold. "You aren't in charge; just because it's your dad doesn't mean shit. How many times do I have to tell you this."

"I'll always be in charge. Get used to it."

I pause for a moment, realizing I should focus on picking my battles wisely. This particular one isn't worth the fight, at least for now.

Twenty-Three

Ashton

I've been running around trying to catch up on classes, while trying to keep an eye on Jinx. She isn't making our life any easier this week ever since Wilde moved Dad to a different location. Atticus is the only one who knows where he's at because he doesn't trust us not to say anything to her. Not that I would, and angry Atticus isn't someone I want around. He's been bitchy ever since leaving the basement. I wish Jinx would listen to what we had to say sometimes. We may not have grown up with our dad, but he isn't someone you want to visit alone. And yes, I realize how stupid that sounds after she spent five days with him, but he could've done anything to her, and he never.

He's unstable. I wish Jinx knew that.

I forgot how much I hate accounting. The only thing that makes it worthwhile is having Jinx next to me. I glance over, and she stares straight ahead, ignoring me like usual.

"The silent treatment doesn't work on me." I rest my head on her shoulder. "It turns me on."

"That's a shame for you, isn't it."

"Jesus. Who shit in your cornflakes?"

She shrugs her shoulder, making me sit up. "If you haven't figured that out, I can't help you."

"If you weren't so stubborn and listened, you would see why Atticus did what he did. You can't fault him for that."

"It's not that. It's the fact that Atticus thinks he can still boss me around. All I wanted was a few simple answers. Where is the box, or did he even have Dad's heart? That's all I wanted."

I wrap my arm around her shoulder, dragging her closer. I work my hand into her hair, giving it a slight tug when I get to the roots. A small moan slips from her mouth, and her head snaps in my direction.

"Looks like I'm not the only one getting turned on." I chuckle.

"Yeah, can you fix that for me?"

"How?" I know she won't pressure me into sex, and deep down, I want to try, but what if I'm not ready?

"It's okay, Ashton. You don't need to."

"No. I want to. Let's go somewhere now." I grab our books and stand. The anticipation for what's to come has my heart racing. I have no idea where to go, but I know it has to be remarkable. I drag her out of the row, getting groans from the other assholes as we pass by. The professor doesn't say anything as we leave. Not that I would listen to him, anyway.

"Ashton, where are we going?"

"I haven't figured that out yet. Pick one, the art building or the music hall."

"Well, we already fucked in the art building."

"My God, woman, the mouth you have."

She laughs. "You haven't complained yet."

And I don't think I ever will. But it's the stubbornness of hers that drives me insane. She needs to start listening more. We quickly exist the main building and run across the courtyard.

"Ash, I don't think this is a good idea. It's going to be super busy in there."

"Don't be so shy. They are making music and soon we will be too."

The last time I was in Greywood Hall was to watch Maddox and Jinx play together. I had high hopes that they would win a spot in the symphony, but I should've known better with Von sleeping with Lola. I'm glad Maddox took him out, but he'll be back unless Allan gets his head out of his ass and hires a new professor.

I haul Jinx to the last door, hoping it's vacant. I twist the doorknob and get lucky. "Get your ass inside."

I push her against the wall, my lips crashing onto her in a desperate kiss. She moans, and her hands tangle in my hair, pulling me closer. As I pull back, I run my hands down her body to the hem of her shirt; pulling off her top, her small, perky breasts are revealed like a Christmas gift. I can't resist bending down and taking a nipple in my mouth, sucking hard. Her moans fill the empty concert hall.

I pull her nipple from my mouth and look up at her. "You like that, don't you?"

"Yeah." Her words came out low, tinged with a sensual edge.

Her body arches towards me, urging me on. My fingers find their way under her skirt, feeling her naked pussy. "Fuck," I growl as I feel how wet she is for me already. I slip a finger inside her tight walls, watching with satisfaction as it slides in and out effortlessly.

With one hand gripping her thigh and the other still working its magic between her legs, I kneel to explore her with my tongue. She tastes sweet and musky, and I can't get enough of her. The sounds of her pleasure fill my ears as I suck on her clit; I dig my fingers into her thigs, burying my face deeper into her pussy, licking into her wet entrance to her clit. Her fingers weave into my hair, pushing me closer, and her leg shakes the more I suck her clit. Her moans grow louder as her hips jerk forward, and she finds her release. Her juices flow onto my face and I revel in it.

I lick my lips, coming up and taking her lips once more. "Taste yourself. Tell me how you taste."

"I'd rather taste you on my lips." She grins and slowly slides her hands down my stomach, stopping at my waistband. She pauses, waiting for me to stop her.

"Get on your knees, Little Grim."

She gracefully kneels before me, anticipation builds in her eyes, a glint of determination as her fingers work quickly, unbuttoning my pants and pulling them down to reveal my throbbing dick. I watch eagerly as her hand reaches for me, wrapping around and guiding me to her mouth; her lips part as she looks up at me.

"I want you to gag on my dick."

Her tongue teasingly flicks the tip, making me groan. My fingers wrap around her hair, urging her on until her nose presses against my skin. I hold her there for a moment, savoring the sensation before she taps my leg and pulls back, taking a deep breath.

"That pretty little face deserves to be fucked."

I watch her eyes dilate and her fingers dig into my thighs. "Please."

In one smooth motion, I push her back onto me, plunging deep into the wet heat of her mouth. My head falls back as I'm lost in pleasure. Jinx moans around each thrust as I fuck her mouth deeper and deeper. Every moment sends shivers down my spine; I pull out when she taps once more, and a trail of drool drips from her chin onto her breasts.

Before I can overthink it, I walk behind her, pushing her onto all fours. My heart races as I kneel behind her; with shaky hands, I flip up her skirt.

"Ash, it's okay if you aren't ready." She tilts her head, watching me carefully.

I slap her ass, and she bows her head, letting out a low moan. "You have such a perfect pussy, Jinx. Yours is the only one I've ever wanted."

Unable to hold back any longer, I slide my throbbing dick inside her. All the anxiety I had for the last two years tried to come slamming back, but this is different; I'm in control and can stop anytime I need to. I close my eyes and feel her wet pussy as I slide back and forth. Her back arches, pressing into me. I grab her hips, thrusting hard.

"Your dick feels so good in my pussy." Jinx moans, dropping her head to the floor.

"Do you want me to make you come?" She moans when I pull out halfway and drive in deep. "Answer me."

"Yes!" She screams.

I sink onto the floor, pulling her with me into reverse cowgirl. "Play with yourself while you fuck me."

Her hips flex forward as her hand disappears between her legs, and her muscles clamp around my dick. She leans back, grinding on my dick, and I'm lost in the rhythm of her body. I reach up and grab her breasts, squeezing them as she rides me. I can't help but groan as she squeezes me again; if only this were my first time, everything else wouldn't matter. I thrust deeper, trying to remove those thoughts. This is where I belong with Jinx and no one else.

Her body starts to tremble and I know she's close. "I want you to come all over my dick." With one final thrust, I push her over the edge, and she comes apart. I feel myself reaching the edge. "Where do you want it?"

"Come in my mouth. I want to taste you."

She climbs off and turns around, taking my dick in her hand, stroking me. I grab her hair. "Open, I'm coming." I slam my dick in her mouth, shooting my cum down her throat. I watch my cum drip from her lips as I pull out, and it's the most satisfying thing I've witnessed.

"God, you're gorgeous." I swipe her lips, sticking my finger in her mouth. Her eyes start to go misty, and I panic. "What's wrong?"

"Nothing. I'm so proud of you, that's all."

I drop my forehead onto hers. "Shit, I don't think any-one has told me that before. Thank you, Jinx, for being so understanding with me."

"Always." She cups my face, tilting it upward before slowly kissing my lips.

"I don't deserve you."

"You do. Don't ever let those demons tell you other-wise. You will always win."

"I'll try. We should leave before someone walks in. I didn't lock the door."

She smacks me. "You asshole, someone could've seen us."

I shrug. "Yeah, that's the fun of it all."

"What is with you, Bank boys and public sex?"

"It's exciting, don't you think?"

She rolls her eyes and grabs her shirt. "What would you do if you did get caught?"

"Make you come while they watch and then beat the shit out of them for watching." I stand and pull my pants up; as I'm butting my pants, the door opens. I look at Jinx and burst into laughter.

"You are fucking lucky, mister."

I grab our bags and her hand. "Yeah, but now they have to sit in here and smell us." As we exit, I come face to face with Cam. I grip Jinx's hand tighter.

"Well, what do we have here?" Cam scoffs as he pushes us back into the concert hall.

"The fuck do you think you're doing?" Jinx spits out, trying to work around me.

"Your whore has to fight your battles now? Maybe I'll take a round out of her now that you loosened her up."

I feel my blood boil; I let go of Jinx, and without thinking, I move fast, swinging my fist into the side of Cam's face. He turns his body, swinging his fist back at me; I dodge it, feeling the familiar adrenaline rush through my veins. We're locked in a violent dance, our fists colliding in a chaotic fury; as we continue to exchange blows, I feel a sense of freedom coursing through me, a release of pent-up frustration from what my dad decided to do to Jinx. And everything I've held in for years; it almost feels like I'm on the outside of my body watching the scene unfold until Cam lands a solid punch to my stomach, sending me to my knees.

"Looks like I win." He bends down and snarls in my face.

"Fuck you," I gasp. I lunge forward, grabbing Cam by the collar and throwing him to the ground; I deliver one last punch to his face, knocking him unconscious. I stay kneeling on the floor, trying to find my breath.

"Ash?" Jinx spoke lowly.

I glance over and spot Jinx clutching her chest, eyes wide with fear. Her mouth hangs open, and she lets out tiny wheezing sounds as her chest rises and falls.

"Where's your inhaler?" I don't wait for her to answer; I look around to where I dropped our bags. I shuffle across the floor, tearing open her bag. I shuffle through all her books, opening pouches. When I open the last pouch I find it. I shake it, flick the end cap off, and run back to Jinx.

"Here, suck it in." She grabs my hand, releases a breath, and takes a puff. "I'm sorry, Jinx. I didn't mean to stress you out."

She shakes her head, takes the inhaler from me, and takes another puff. "You didn't," she manages to say. "It all caught up to me finally."

"I'll take it easier on you next time." I drag her into my chest.

"Please, don't I like it when you don't hold back. I get the real you. But what are we gonna do with Cam?"

I glance down at a passed-out Cam. "Fuck him, he had no right coming in here in the first place. Leave him for someone else to find. Let him go crying to his granddaddy."

"That reminds me, I have a meeting with the board members this week."

"Lovely. I'm sure Archer will enjoy that." I release her and take her hand, guiding her back toward the door, stopping to grab our shit. "What about Roan? Will he be there?"

"He's supposed to be there; I hope he doesn't show up. He was an asshole last time."

"You never did tell us about the meeting; you know that right." It's been on the back of my mind since I walked into that boardroom. I should've known Roan was up to something even then. I wouldn't put it past him to commit a murder.

I only need that motive.

Twenty-Four

Jinx

I still haven't seen Edgar, and my heart breaks every day that he doesn't make his appearance. I don't want to believe he would leave me, but I'm beginning to think that's how it's going. The twins have a swim practice today, and Maddox and Wilde are doing their thing. It's almost as if things are back to normal around here. I would like to believe that, but something is missing.

Pencil: Teeny, come on, I'm hungry

I turn, slip my phone off the nightstand, and stare at the text. Fuck. I forgot I promised Spence I would head to the food court to grab something to eat with him. He's been dragging me out of the dorm almost every chance he's gotten.

Pencil: Get the fuck out of bed, I'm coming in

I groan, throwing the blanket over my head. I'm not in the mood for people. The board meeting is tomorrow, and I'm not ready to face Roan. Allan called me saying he'll be there, but that doesn't help me either, and now, with Cameron out for blood again, Archer will be in a screaming match.

"Jinx, I know you're under the blanket. You can't hide from me."

The mattress dips, and Spence pulls the blanket back before getting under it. We're engulfed in darkness and silence. My eyes slowly adjust to the darkness, and my beautiful friend comes into view.

"Hey."

"Hey, yourself. Start talking, what's the matter?"

I roll onto my back, tossing the blanket off my head. "It's the same shit. Who killed Dad? Where did Atticus place his Dad? I want some answers, but no one is giving them to me."

Spence rolls onto his side, wrapping his arm around my stomach and laying his head on my shoulder. "I can't help you with any of that on an empty stomach."

I smack his arm. "My God. It's not always about that stomach."

"It is. I might be able to help with the Atticus issue."

I lean away and stare at him. "How?"

He points to his mouth. Oh my God, he's relentless. I kick the blankets off us and sit up. "Fine, but you owe me every juicy detail you have."

He salutes me. "Aye, aye, captain."

I climb out of bed and find my fanny pack lying on the floor. "Are you getting up or not?" I ask as I strap my pack on.

"Yeah, just enjoying the view."

"Pig. How's River?"

He rolls out of bed and flips me the finger. "That's a low blow. She only used me for my fantastic dick skills and then left me. I knew that's what she was after, but deep down, I didn't want to believe it."

"You were also using her for the big tits, so." I shrug, leaving the room.

He scrambles after me. "That's not the same thing," he bursts out.

"Okay, whatever you need to tell yourself. But you didn't complain about her before."

"You know what, I'll complain about her now. She hurt Spencey's feelings."

"Your dick is fine."

"You know it is." He laughs when he steps out of the dorm.

If I ever have to see his dick again, I'll chop it off. I have my boundaries, but Spence loves to test them. One day, he'll test them too far and won't like what he'll get in return.

"Can you tell me about Atticus now?" The anticipation is killing me, and I need to know.

Spence opens the door for the stairs and looks down at me. "No. I know you. You'll back out on food, and I'm not that stupid. We shall discuss it while we eat."

"I hate how well you know me."

"Same."

We exit Greywood, and the cold wild hits me. Why he wanted to leave some place warm is beyond me. The bed was so much nicer.

"I heard a rumor going around school."

"Oh?" I can only imagine what sort of rumor is being spread. I'm gonna go with Cam. Spence keeps quiet, building the suspense. I nudge my elbow into his ribs, making him squeal.

"My God. Fine. I heard a new music professor was hired. No more dealing with Von and his bullshit. You might have a chance after all."

If only the damage hadn't already been done. It's too late for me. I've accepted my fate; perhaps playing music professionally isn't for me. Von ruined that for me, and I'll never be able to forgive him for that.

"That's great and all, but useless none of the same." The food court is crowded with students trying to escape the cold. I glare at Spence, but he acts like he doesn't notice.

"Grab a seat, and I'll grab the food."

"I hate you."

"Love you too, Teeny."

I leave him and try to find a table away from prying ears. I feel like everyone is watching me as I weave around the tables. I try my hardest to ignore them, but the hairs on my neck raise as I sit, facing the entrance. I pull my phone out, trying to look busy, and ignore all the stares. A shadow falls upon the table. I peer up from my phone and see Lola standing at the table's edge.

"Can I help you?" Giving her a board look.

"Yeah, you can. What the fuck did you do with Von?"

"Why would you think I had anything to do with him?" I lean back, crossing my arms.

She slams her hands on the table, leaning closer. "Don't act like no one knows. We know you own this school. Same last name as the dead dean. It's not hard to put two and two together. Now get my Von back."

I can't help but laugh in her face and lean in close. "If you know I own this school, you should be extremely fucking worried that I don't mess with your music career that you so sucked your way to the top. One call, and you're finished."

"You wouldn't dare."

I raise an eyebrow, daring her to try whatever she has planned.

"What's going on, ladies?" Spencer slams his food tray on the table, scaring Lola. "The teacher fuckers eat over there in case you're lost." He tilts his head to the other side of the room.

"You two can go to hell."

"Nah, we'll leave that for you." Spence sits, handing me my food, not caring if Lola is still hanging around. He looks up at Lola. "Still here?"

She huffs. "My God, don't you care about Von?"

"No." We both answer.

She finally takes the hint and walks away. I take the wrap off the tray and start unwrapping it. "Alright, spill, I'm eating, you're eating. Tell me everything."

"Jesus, Jinx. Give me a moment to actually start eating. The tummy needs the fuel to deal with you."

I let him get a bite of his burger and tap my fingers on the table. He rolls his eyes and chews slower. I'm about to climb over this table and ram that burger in his face.

"Ready to know my intel?"

"Yes! My God. Spill the beans."

"Okay, calm down. I ran into that Wilde dude the other day, and we started talking. Turns out he's a pretty cool guy. He's into gaming, too. We started talking about the latest game and how I should stream it."

"Spence. Atticus."

"Yeah. I'm getting there." He deadpans. "He asked how I knew the guys, so I told them that they are slipping their dicks into my bestie."

I choke on my food. "Excuse me?"

"You heard me. That's beside the point. He gave me some ideas. Let me love the guy. He eventually told me about the twin's Dad." He takes another bite of his burger. "He told me where he is."

"If it's the old administration building, they moved him."

"It's not. He's not on RWA property."

"Where the fuck is he? I need to see him."

"I'll take you there if you want, but it has to be now while the twins are busy. I'm not gonna be responsible for any of this shit when they find out. Tell them you're heading to the city."

I open the group text, sending a message to all three of the guys, telling them that I'm going to the city with Spence for something to do. I take another bite of my food. When my phone dings.

Maddox: Be safe, don't do anything stupid

I don't expect the twins to reply if they are in a meeting. But I'm sure they will after the fact.

Me: Nothing stupid, just some shopping for Spence.

"Roll out before they catch onto our shenanigans."

Wherever they moved him isn't somewhere I'm familiar with, but I'm glad Spence knows. I'm also pleased he's taking me; at least he understands what I need. We turn down a backroad, and my nerves ride high. What if I get answers that aren't what I want? If he only wanted to be closer to his sons, he went the wrong way about doing so. I don't understand stalking someone and tormenting them.

Spence turns and makes another turn, and I pray he doesn't get lost. "Are you ready for this? I'll be there the entire time, but if you aren't, we can turn back."

"I'm good. I need this, and maybe the guys also need this; they just don't know it yet."

"If you say so. I swear if he says the wrong thing, Jinx, I won't hesitate."

"I know." I stare out my window, watching the trees zip by, hoping I made the right decision again. I have to remind myself I'm not alone this time around, and nothing will happen.

"What's the plan, Teeny?"

"I don't know. I have no idea what he looks like or what to expect. This could be a waste of my time."

Spence turns down another road, slowing down. "This is the spot; we can turn back if you want."

"No. We never back down from a task, we can't start now."

An old barn looms in front of us, the chipping red paint and broken boards blending in with the vibrant red and orange foliage enveloping it. Spence parks the car, and my heart pounds in my chest. This is the last thing I need to do, but talking with my stalker is going to be hard, especially with the twins not knowing. I take a deep breath and open the door, stepping out into the chilly air. Spence follows suit, his curious eyes darting around the abandoned barn.

"I'll ask again. Are you sure?"

"I'm positive."

With a sense of determination, I lead Spence toward the entrance. As we near the doors, I can feel my heart race faster, but I can't back down. Not now, not after everything that has happened. Spence places his hand on the door, and with a nod, he slides it open.

A shadowy figure sits on a bale of hay in the corner of the barn.

"Jinx, are you fucking kidding me? The city, my God-damn ass. I can't believe you would come out here. I can't believe this shit. And you." Atticus stands, storming toward us. "I should beat the shit out of you for bringing her out here."

"A swim meeting. Who's the fucking liar?" I step in front of Spencer.

"If I told you I was coming to see him, you would've begged and pleaded to come."

"Yeah, and you would've said no 'cause you think you're the boss. So I found a different way."

He leans in close to my face. "I should smack the shit out of you."

I get closer until our noses touch. "Fucking try it."

"Okay! That's enough." Spence grabs me, pulling me away from Atticus. "If this is going to be an issue, I can take her back."

"Atticus, I need this, and you know it. And I didn't come alone this time, which should mean something."

He closes his eyes and then looks at Spencer. "Fine, but Spence, you can't be here. I don't wanna be an asshole or anything, but Ash is in there with him right now, and it's gonna be a little emotional, and I don't think he wants anyone to see him like that."

"Hey, I get it. But I'm not leaving. I'll be in the car in case something happens." He places a kiss on my forehead and walks away.

I look at Atticus. "If you fucking threaten me again, it'll be you that's begging. Do you hear me?"

He raises a blond brow. "My brother finally fucks you, and you suddenly grow a pair. Is this how it works now?"

"Jealous because it took him to do the job?"

He steps closer, grabbing my hair and weaving his fingers between the strands. "No, Little Grim. Because when we get back, I'll make sure all three of us show you that we're all in charge."

I hate how he always thinks he's in charge. Not this time around. I reach out and grab his dick, giving it a squeeze. "If anything, Atticus. I'm in charge."

His blue eyes lock onto mine. "Is that so?" he growls, his voice low and dangerous.

I tighten my grip on him, feeling him harden beneath my palm. "That's right," I say, my voice steadier than I feel.

He pulls my hair, forcing my head at an angle, exposing my neck. I gasp as he trails kisses down my neck, his free hand sliding under my shirt, fingers dancing across my skin.

"Still think you're in charge?" he whispers, nipping at my neck.

I bite my lip, trying to suppress my moan. I refuse to bend to him; I move my hand along his hard dick, gaining my control back. "Maybe we should find out," I challenge.

"Fuck, Jinx. It's been so long since I felt you." He nips at my neck again, and my pussy grows wet, aching for his touch.

"Hate to break up the fuck feast, but the asshole wants to talk to you, Ace."

My world comes crashing back to me.

Twenty-Five

Atticus

Fuck.

I've been dreading this since that day. I pull away from Jinx and look over at Ash, and his eyes were distant. Whatever that prick said to him can't be good. Jinx lets go of me and goes to Ash, embracing him in her arms. As he looks at me over her head, tears are on the brink of falling from his eyes.

I try to find a calming breath, but nothing comes of it. I glance at the room where he's at and know I have to head in there, if not for my own sake but for Ash and Jinx's sake. I cross the old barn and stop at the door. I glance back at Ash and Jinx. Jinx is still hugging Ash, but she moves her head and fixes me with a gentle look. I know whatever happens, she'll be here for me.

The door creaks open as I push it forward. The man I haven't seen in years is tied to a chair in the far dark corner. I take a deep breath and prepare myself for the conversation ahead. I grab a chair and place it directly in front of him; his dark eyes glare at me as I sit.

"Took you long enough, thought I would die before I got to see you. The other one is too sensitive. I blame your mother. Guess I should've asked for you instead."

My fingers coil into a tight fist on my thighs. "You know nothing about Ashton."

He laughs. "I know plenty. You think I wouldn't learn a thing or two after watching you for all these months? I know one thing, you two can't keep your dick in your pants. I also wouldn't think of you guys as the type to sleep with your new sister. What kind of children did your mother raise?"

"Better than what you would've done, trust me." I can feel my blood boiling, but this conversation isn't getting me anywhere. "Tell me. Why now?"

"It's simple. I'm surprised you haven't figured it out already."

With a swift movement, I launch myself at him and deliver a powerful blow to his stomach. His body lurches forward, desperate for air. I seize a handful of his silvering hair and forcefully yank his head back, his eyes widening in fear as he sees my fist approaching.

"Wait, I'll talk," he gasps, closing his eyes when I stop at his nose.

"Smart fucking answer, Augustus. I won't think twice about spilling your blood." I move back to my chair, rage ringing deep in my bones. How the fuck am I supposed to know why he's back and after Ashton.

"I got word when you both started at Ravenwood Academy; I'll admit pride washed over me."

"Trust me, you had nothing to do with it."

"I'm aware. Serena made it difficult for me to visit; don't think I didn't try."

This is annoying; he's prolonging shit, and I'm about to walk out and say fuck it. "You have five minutes, and then I'm leaving."

He leans his head back like he's trying to recall a memory. "Like I was saying, I got word that you two enrolled here and knew there was money to be had. Your mother wasn't always wise when it came to men, but this time, she hit it. I knew this was my chance, and what do you know, I know someone on the board."

"Who?" I stand, my heart thumping hard.

"Roan Grant."

I feel like the rug has been yanked out from under me. My ears ring, drowning out any noise, and I can't catch my breath. He's been friends with Roan all along. Was this a setup? I need to talk with Ash. I can't do this one alone. I can't look at him. I push the chair back, and it topples to the floor with a bang. I walk to the door, and his words play in my head. Roan Grant. He's friends with Roan.

"Atticus? What's wrong?" Jinx comes running to me, locking her arms around my stomach.

I wrap my arms around her shoulders. "I um. Need to talk to you and Ash."

"What did he say to you?" Ashton asks, his voice echoing in the barn.

I look for him and find him sitting on the hay bale, his head in his hands. I move both of us to his side, indicating that Jinx should sit.

"I don't think I like where this is going." Her teeth bite her lip as she sits close to Ashton.

I run my hand through my hair, feeling a bit frustrated. Why did I have to find this out? No point dragging it out, this shit has been going on for months, and it needs to end today.

"Seems like Roan wasn't working alone at the school."

Ashton stands, already reading into that sentence. "Are you fucking kidding me?"

"I wish I was."

"I don't understand. Your dad knows Roan?"

Ash drops his hand on her shoulder. "Seems so. What else did he say?"

"He knew money was involved; now, I don't know if that means he had his hand in Prescott's murder, but if I had to say anything, I'm going with Roan, him and Mother planned it so they could get a huge payout."

"You don't think. Do you?" She stares up at me, her green eyes growing a darker shade. "Let me in that room, Atticus."

"Ace, let her. He's tied to a chair. He can't get to her."

"You stay by my side. If anything, I don't like is said, you are in that car with Spencer. Don't fight me, Jinx. I can't take it today."

"I promise. I only want answers, that's all."

I'm going to regret this. I know it. After this, Jinx can stop nagging me to see him, and I can finally write him out of my life for good. There isn't anything for him anymore. He can't go after her once he discovers Mother didn't get a dime. And if he was a part of murdering Prescott, one call to the cops and his ass will be in jail for life. Either way, I don't have to deal with him.

I escort Jinx to the room, but before she can enter, I block her way. "I swear, Jinx. One wrong word, and you're out. You thought I was an asshole, he's worse. I don't even want Ash back in here."

"I understand. What else is there to be said? I just want some truth. Living without answers is worse than anything. I need to be able to move on, that's all."

"Okay. I trust you." I move out of her way and enter first. "Jinx, meet the asshole that stalked you, Augustus."

He looks over at her and grins. "Mmm, my favorite prey. How have you been?"

"You shut the fuck up, or I'll break your jaw." Jinx places her hand on my arm, calming me slightly.

"It's alright. I don't believe he was my stalker."

"What makes you say that?"

Jinx walks closer until she's standing in front of him. "Because my stalker never called me Doll, and the things he said he wanted to do to me, he sure had the chance but never did. You are nothing to me. But I'm gonna go out on a limb and say Roan is the real stalker."

He gave a little throaty laugh. "Wow, give the lady a fucking reward. She figured it out. Took you long enough."

"What about my dad? What did you do to him?" She hauls off and smacks him across the face. The crack vibrates off the walls.

He jerks in the chair, trying to break free. "You bitch!" he screams. "You expect me to tell you anything now? Why don't you call him and see what he says?" He grins, thinking he's smug as shit.

"No. I have a better plan. Guess you'll have to sit and rot here a little bit longer." She backs away, reaching for me and squeezing my hand. She tilts her head back. "I'm gonna go. Do you two need a ride back?"

"No. Maddox is coming back, and I feel like tormenting this prick a little longer."

She hesitates, looking back at Augustus. "Are you sure? I don't trust him."

"He's tied to a chair; he can't do anything."

"No, but that mouth of his can." She pulls me down by the neck. "Ashton isn't doing so good," she whispers in my ear.

"I know. I'll talk to Ashton after. We're all gonna need time to deflect from this shit. I promise Ash will be fine." I brush her hair away, cupping the back of her neck. "And you know I never break my promises."

"Okay. Call me if you need anything, and I'll come back."

I watch as she disappears before turning back to him. "You fucking prick. You're the mastermind behind everything, aren't you?"

His nostrils flare, and his jaw tenses. "I might be. You don't think your mother could pull this off. She married the guy, after all."

"No. She's fucking dense. Either it was you or Roan, and I have my suspicions it was you. What I remember about you the most is that you always wanted money, and if you are friends with Roan, that explains everything."

"It explains nothing. You think you figured it out; you haven't even reached the tip of the iceberg. Son." A grin of amusement pulled at the corner of his mouth.

"Don't Son me. You lost that title when you walked out. And after what you did to Jinx, never call me that again."

He scoffs, leaning as far forward as he can. "I'm not worried. Your little girlfriend still has to deal with Roan, and I would be more concerned about that more than anything. I'm not the bad guy here. He's the one who stalked her, took pictures of her, and, if I'm correct, has a meeting with her tomorrow."

Fuck.

I can't let her be in that meeting. I have a sneaking suspicion that Roan will try something. I leave the room and find Ashton.

"When is Maddox coming? I need to get the fuck out of here."

Me: We need to leave, when can you get here?

"I sent him a text. We can step outside if you need a breather. I'm done talking to the asshole."

"Please. If I stay here any longer, it won't end well."

I shouldn't have allowed Ash to talk to him. Whatever was said in that room should'nt of been said, and if I know that cunt, he degraded Ashton until he was nothing but an ant on the floor. Ashton is calm but is sensitive when being yelled at. Like anyone would be, he'll never tell me what was said; he'll bottle it up until he explodes.

"How bad did he fuck her up?" He digs a joint from his pocket and lights it.

"It's a combination of Roan and Mother, too." He takes a puff before handing it to me. "Roan's the stalker, and I'm sure everyone had a part in Prescott's murder." I take a deep puff, feeling the sweet herb fill my lungs.

"What's the plan now?"

"I'm not sure. Jinx mentioned a plan, and that makes me nervous. Her and her plans don't always work out."

"She doesn't leave our side once we get back. I don't care what she says."

If I know Jinx, she's going to go after Mother.

Twenty-Six

Jinx

I shouldn't be this nervous. But knowing I have to face a room full of men tomorrow morning is freaking me out. It also doesn't help that I'm stuck between the twins while they are passed out. They are making it impossible for me to get out of bed. I need to get things off my mind.

I stare at the ceiling for another ten minutes before I give in. I pull the blankets back, and Atticus grumbles, moving his arm looking for them. I carefully climb over him, and his eyes snap open.

"Little Grim? Going somewhere?" his voice came out horse and broken.

"Yeah. To pee, do you mind." I sass him.

He tilts his head in a yes motion. Like I need his permission, I climb off him and leave the bedroom. I head for the living room and open the window, hoping that Edgar will come by. I stare into the darkness, wishing he would come by now. I need my friend back. A surge of disappointment runs through my body when he doesn't show. I turn and find my cello in the stand next to my seat.

I run my hand along the neck, feeling the smooth wood. My skin prickles with happiness to have it back in my hands again. I pick up my bow and settle the cello comfortably between my legs as I take a seat. I adjust the bow in my hand, position my fingers, and begin to play. My body sways as the melody takes me away. This is what I needed to relax.

"Gwah."

My body freezes. I swing around to the window and there he sits. I drop my cello and rush over to him.

"Edgar." I hiccup, tears falling on the counter. "Where have you been?" I hold my hand out, waiting for him to step on my palm.

"Kraa."

"I know, it's been ages. Did you have grand adventures?" I stroke his head, and he nuzzles into it more. "God, I've missed you." I cradle him into my chest, needing him closer.

"Jinx?"

I turn around and see a blurry Ashton standing in front of me. "He came back." I sniff, trying not to break down completely.

"Come here, love." He holds his arms open, inviting me in.

"He's back."

Ashton pets Edgar on the head, and he looks up at Ashton. "Kraa."

"Yeah, missed you too, buddy. But if you leave her again. It's roast chicken out of you."

I pull Edgar closer. "He's kidding; I would never let him do that." I look at Ash. "Don't say such things. He's sensitive."

"Are you two finished? I'm tired. Put the bird down."

"Kraa."

"Yeah, he's still an asshole." I pull away from Ash and glare at Atticus. "Don't be a dick." I place Edgar back on the counter and watch as he hops closer to the window. My heart sinks when he shakes his feathers out.

"He'll come back, Jinx."

I turn back to Atticus, and he simply nods. "Okay, I trust you." With one more squawk, Edgar flies away. I feel like a part of me has left with him. I can only hope that Atticus is right and Edgar will come back.

"You okay? I heard you playing." Ashton rubs my lower back as I continue to stare out the window.

"Yeah, I need to calm my mind."

"Nervous about tomorrow?" Atticus asks.

I turn, crossing my arms, and take them in. "What if Roan says something, and I'm unprepared to answer it? I know Allan will be there, so I'm not overly worried, but it still scares me."

After what he said to me last time, I won't put it past him for saying something this time around. And now that I know he's been stalking me, how am I supposed to look at him? He's seen so much my privacy doesn't exist to him. My skin crawls at the thought of it. He was in my dorm room and also left me those roses. I take a deep breath, trying to calm myself.

"Shit, Jinx. Steady your breathing. In and out." Ashton cups my face and breathes with me. "Good, you've got this."

When my chest isn't tight anymore, I drop my head on his chest. "I don't want to do this."

"No one says you have to, but you're stubborn and will do it, anyway. Whatever you have planned, Jinx it better work."

"It will, Atticus. Have some faith in me for once."

"You should try to get some sleep. Tomorrow is gonna drain the fuck out of you," Ashton speaks into my hair.

I take a deep breath and smooth down my dress again. I don't want to do this. I stare at myself in the mirror, taking in my appearance. Spending five days in that basement took a toll on me; my body doesn't look like mine still. I want the old Jinx back.

"Jinx, we gotta go." Atticus knocks on the bathroom door.

I take one more inhale and give myself a nod. "You are a bad bitch." I open the door to find Atticus and Ashton wearing a suit each. I point at them. "Explain."

"We are going to that meeting. If you think we're letting you sit in that room alone, you can forget about it. Maddox is also joining us."

"Ashton, no. You three can't be there. The things we discuss are not for the general public."

"Oh, so were the general public now?"

I throw my hands in the air. "Yes."

"Tough luck, we're going. Now grab your pack, and let's go." Atticus turns, and I can't help but stare at him. How can an asshole look that good in a suit?

"Yeah, we look pretty fuckin' hot in these, don't we?" Ashton grabs his lapel and pulls them, looking smug.

"Whatever, I don't have time for your macho ego." I move past him, grabbing my fanny pack and jacket. The sooner I get in that meeting, the quicker it'll be over. I don't talk to either guy as I step into the hall, but when

I see Maddox in dress pants and shirt, it's the leather jacket that seals the deal for me.

"Baby. Are you ready?"

"Yeah, if we hurry up and stop asking that question."

"Deal." He grabs my hand, intertwining our fingers. The twins lead the way, and I try not to think of what I want to do with them while they wear those suits. You can barely see Atticus' neck tattoos peaking over the collar of his dress shirt, adding to the mystery of what's underneath.

I'll never get used to this cold air; bring back the autumn warmth. Maddox never lets go of my hand the entire walk across the courtyard. But the closer we get to the school, the more I regret this meeting. I should've canceled it even if this needs to be done and dealt with.

As we walk into the school, Florence meets us. "They started the meeting early. You didn't get my message?"

"What? No. Those assholes. I should've known they would've done this." I let go of Maddox's hand and storm toward the boardroom, and if I have to say whose idea it was, I'm going to go with Roan. Why wouldn't Allan reach out to me? He knew I had to be there. I turn down the hall, and Allan is waiting.

"Odette. Thank God. It's a shitshow in there. They won't listen to me, and I have no idea what the hell is going on."

"It's fine, Allan. They all have massive egos and love to bitch. It's who they are." I turn to the guys. "You can't come in. I don't care what you say."

"Jinx." Atticus growls.

"She's correct, boys. You can't be in that room without authority. School rules, and believe me, I didn't make them."

"What stupid rule is that?" Ashton scoffs.

"Yes, well, it's not a normal school if you haven't noticed. So, if you don't mind, Odette and I will be going in." Allan opens the door, extending a hand for me to enter first.

"If I need you, I'll yell."

"Fuckin' rights you will. I'm breaking down the doors if I hear one peep from you." Maddox looked at me; his left eye twitched.

I give them a nod and step into the room from hell. Allan slams the door behind us, and the room falls quiet. Barnaby sits at the table, resting his folded hands in front of him. Archer halts his step before his chair, and when my eyes land on Roan, I need to steady my breath. His brown eyes latch onto mine, and the last few months have come flooding back. Everything he's done to me is like a rush. I turn back to Burnaby, the netural party at the table.

"Good morning, Burnaby."

"Miss Hawthorne. How are you?"

I take the seat at the head, establishing my power over the room. I do my best not to look at Roan when he sits beside me. Allan sits on my other side, followed by Archer.

"Can we start with the fact that my grandson was found unconscious in the concert hall."

I have to hold in my laugh. That asshole had it coming. "And why was Cameron there in the first place, Archer? He isn't even in music to begin with."

Archer lays his eyes on me. "I don't think that matters. Someone beat him up, and he won't say who. I want justice."

"Cameron is a big boy. He can handle his shit. Maybe you should let him for once. Can we move on?" I lean back in my chair, waiting for Archer to argue like always.

"I can accept that. I do need to let Cameron figure out his battles. It's hard for me sometimes, you know."

I resist the temptation to clean my ears because I don't think I heard what I did. Did Archer agree with me? This isn't happening; he's always fought back. Cameron was his precious little boy that couldn't do any harm. What the fuck is happening?

"That's very mighty of you, Archer. Thank you," Burnaby speaks up.

"Yes, mighty," Roan drawled, looking bored.

"Do you have something to add, Roan?" Archer snaps back.

I'm not sure if I like where this is headed.

"I do have something to say to Odette." He turns, and I know he's going to air everything.

"And what is that, Roan? I'm still confused what you bring to this school."

His lip curves into a sinister smile. "I'm the money back to this school, Odette. Do you think this school would be operational without me? Think again. I've been here before your father took over. I'm not going to let some girl tell me what to do. Hiring Allan without informing the board goes against the rules.

"Are you kidding me?" Allan's mouth falls open.

"He has to be. You had your time to bring this up after Dad died. Why wait?"

There's no way this is what he wanted to talk about. He's got to be dense. How does he not know I cracked the stalker code? It's been days since Wilde took Augustus and hid him; Roan hasn't been able to contact him; I need to figure out his angle.

"I figured a meeting with everyone was the perfect timing to bring it up and have a proper voting."

"Roan, no one cares that Allan is here. He's been doing his job like any other dean would be doing. Just drop it." Burnaby shakes his head.

"I have to agree with Burnaby. Whatever you're trying to start isn't working," Archer adds.

I smile at Roan. "I guess we have our answer. Because I vote the same, and that's three against one. What else do we need to talk about?"

"I believe that's everything, Odette. Meeting adjourns." Burnaby finishes writing his notes, stands, looks at Roan, and clears his throat. "That includes you, Roan. Leave."

Roan glares at me as he backs away from the table. "Don't worry. I know where she is if I need to have a conversation with her again."

Shivers race down my spine; of course, he knows where I am. But the one thing he doesn't know is that his identity has been figured out, and I can't wait to finally catch him in a trap.

Twenty-Seven

Maddox

Jinx told us that Roan wasn't overly threatening in the meeting, but how he spoke to her spooked her. I can't blame her; knowing what she does, I'm surprised she attended that meeting. I would've lost my shit and painted the walls red. Roan wouldn't be breathing.

Wilde has been staying at the barn with the twin's dad. He doesn't fully trust him and swears someone will try to break him free. No matter what we told him, no one knows where Augustus is. But he won't listen. I think a little paranoia is creeping in from his past.

"Jinx, I need to know this plan that you keep talking about." I make eye contact with her once more.

"Don't worry about it. I have it all figured out." She smirks and shoves a chip in her mouth.

I stare at her and wonder who the fuck she is. This isn't the same person that we once knew. Wherever the old Jinx went, she can stay there. I like this fisty one. But her planning skills have never worked out. Well, that's a lie—great planning, but poorly executed.

"Seriously, Jinx. The plan. You need help, and you know it." Ashton reaches over her head and steals a handful of chips from her bowl.

"I do not." She smacks his hand.

"Keep telling yourself that, but it's the truth," Atticus tells her. "I think the only thing that worked out was your accidental divorce plan between Prescott and Mother."

"I didn't mean for that to happen, but I'm glad Dad realized what a witch she was before he died."

"We know, baby. But it was for the best either way."

She takes another chip and stares off in the distance. "I wanted to meet with Serena and Roan privately."

"Nope."

"Fuck that."

"Ain't fucking happening."

She continues like we haven't interrupted her. "To tell her that she can have the school."

"Are you crazy!"

"Why would you do that?"

"Sweet fucking Jesus."

She exhales. "And when Roan thinks he finally broke me, I'll strike. Wilde will haul your dad in, and their gig is up."

"That's your plan?" Ashton asked, his words coming out judgemental.

She tilts her head backward. "Yeah, why?" She shifts so she can face him.

"There's only one hole in that plan. Serena can sniff a fucking lie from a mile away. She'll know you won't give her the school. You've been fighting her on it from day one. Why would you suddenly have a change of heart?"

"Because I'm young and I can't handle it. I think that's a good reason; honestly, it's not a lie. How the fuck am I supposed to be in charge of a school?"

"Jinx, you have us three behind you the whole time. We wouldn't let you fail." Ashton cups her face. "I promise."

"I know, but it's still in the back of my mind."

"And that's okay, no one is saying you can't have those thoughts," I remind her.

She goes back to eating. And I can't help but think of her plan. It could work. Serena is only after money, and Roan wants power and status. But trying to get them to admit to murder that's the tricky thing. Having Augustus show up won't prove much, except Roan stalked her, and we still need to know why. I have my suspicions as to why he did. Scare her away from the school, but why wait until the twins show up? That's what I don't understand. Did

Serena think having them here would make Jinx an easier target?

"When are you following through with your plan?" I need to know because if I know her, it will be tomorrow.

"Tomorrow. I figured, why wait? We can meet at Dad's."

"Leave it to you. I'll call Wilde and get shit figured out."

I leave them alone and head to my dorm. It's not like there is a lot to plan, but trying to escort a fucking asshole can get a little tricky if he decides to fight.

Wilde's phone rings twice before it connects. "Hey, Maddy. How's life in the castle?"

"Oh, you know, peaches and all that."

"Yeah, I bet it is. This barn life might be it for me. It's perfect out here, peaceful, no one to bother you, and I can piss wherever I want."

I can't help but laugh. "The freedom of the land."

"You know it, Maddy. What did you need?"

"We need to move dickwad tomorrow. Jinx has a plan that involves him."

"Okay. I sense something else is wrong."

Him and that spidey sense. I don't trust any of this, and that's the problem. "What if something happens when we get Augustus to the house? I don't trust Roan."

"If that happens, I would be amazed. This cunt proba- bly can't even walk. I've only been giving him enough that he can't pass out. Roan would have to drag him out. He'll be tied to a chair. I'm not worried."

"You don't worry about anything, and that's what scares me. Alright, I'll text you a time tomorrow. If you need anything, let me know."

"Will do."

The line goes dead, and I hope this plan works because I want it all to end. I head back to the twins' dorm when something catches my eye, a black piece of paper on the floor. I bend down and grab it. The golden lettering is addressed to Odette Hawthorne. I turned it around and noticed *DCM* stamped in shiny gold wax, keeping it shut tight.

I enter the door code, still trying to figure out where this came from. "Jinx, something arrived for you."

She tilts her head over the arm of the couch. "What is it?" I hold up the envelope; she sits up, and her eyebrows furrow. "I'm not opening that. The last time a mystery gift was dropped off, it was from *Unknown*."

"You think Roan did this?"

"I don't know. Open it."

I look at the wax seal before breaking it. The flap pops open, and I look at Jinx. "Are you sure you don't want to do this?"

"Yeah, if it's from him, I can't do it again."

I slip the paper out, and my heart punches me in the chest. If this is from Roan, he has some sort of sick game. The envelope drops to the floor, and I carefully unfold the paper. I stare at Jinx.

"Baby, I think you'll want to read this one."

"Why?" Her voice raises a notch.

"Trust me. Where's the guys?"

"They went for a smoke; they should be back soon."

I walk around the couch, staring at Jinx. She's going to be so shocked when she reads this letter. Maybe this is what she needs. A fucking break. God, I'm so proud of her. I drop the letter on the couch and grab her chin.

"You've seen me at my worst and never gave up on me. I don't know what I would do without you, but please never give up on your dreams. Don't let anyone hold you back, not even me."

"What are you saying? You would never hold me back. Maddox, you've helped me so much that I can't express it. I want the best for you, too. I'm proud of you, you've come so far this month." Her hand reaches up and lightly strokes my scar. "You've come so far from this also."

I grab her hand and move it to my mouth, kissing her palm. "A life lesson that I'll forever remember." She moves forward, pressing her lips to mine and wrapping her other hand around my neck, pulling me closer. The feeling of her mouth was almost too intense; I pull away, dropping my forehead to hers. "I'll never get enough of you."

"I hope that feeling never ends."

Her green eyes pierce deep within my soul, sending warm shivers throughout my body. There isn't anything

I wouldn't do for her to feel this when I stare at her. Knowing she's the only soul for me. "If for some reason that feeling ends, I'll find you again and do this all over again. There isn't anything I wouldn't do to keep loving you."

A silent tear rolls down her cheek. "Well, shit." She laughs, whipping her tears away. "I don't even know what to say after that."

"You don't need to. I can see everything I need to."

She wraps her arms around me, "I love you, too. Maddox," she whispers.

The door swings open, and Ashton smiles at me. "What's going on, you two love birds?"

I pull away, caressing Jinx's chin, and grab the letter. "This came for her, and it's best she reads it in front of all of us."

"What is it?" Atticus narrows his eyes.

"Nothing terrible, I swear. And definitely not from Roan."

"Good." Ashton claps his hands. "Read it, sweet cheeks."

She laughs. "You haven't called me that in months."

"I know, but that doesn't mean I haven't thought about those cheeks." He wiggles his brows.

I hand her the letter.

With a deep inhale, she unfolds the letter, and her mouth drops open. "Get the fuck out of here." She pulls the letter to her chest and looks at me.

"What?" Atticus moves closer.

"Jinx, what the fuck is it?" Ashton moves behind her.

I nod. "Yeah, baby. You did it."

"Will somebody start talking," Ace demands.

"It's from the Darwin School of Music. It's an acceptance letter."

Ashton jumps over the couch, crushing her into his chest. "Get the fuck out of here. Congratulations."

She laughs. "Right, but how?"

"Who the fuck cares. You did it." Atticus drops to his knees and wraps her and Ashton in an embrace. "Fuck, Odette, your dream is coming true."

"I did it. Oh, my God." She bursts into tears.

"Yeah, you did, baby."

She reaches for me. "I'm sorry, Maddox. It was your dream also."

"No, it was yours. You've been talking about it your entire life. Go make something of yourself, and we'll be cheering from the crowd."

"Fuckin' rights we will. Everyone will know who Odette Hawthorne is and her crazy ass boyfriends." Ash chuckles.

"Oh, sweet baby Jesus."

Now, we only have to deal with one more issue, and we can finally move on with our lives.

Twenty-Eight

Jinx

I never thought I would be getting answers on who killed Dad.

I knew this day was coming, but now that it's here, I don't know what to expect. What if this doesn't go how I envisioned it? Serena could say something completely different. Maddox drove us to Dad's after breakfast, and now it's up to me to set the bait.

The twins can't sit still, and I swear they are going to wear a hole in the floor of the living room. Each minute I don't make the call, they glare at me. They don't understand the feeling of having to call the one person you despise and know the feeling is mutual.

"Call, Odette." Atticus snaps at me.

"I will, just… give me a second." I tap my phone in my palm, trying to hype myself up. Don't think about it, just dial the phone number. I turn the screen on and find her name in my contacts. I tap *Evil Stepmother* and put the phone to my ear.

"Odette, what brings the pleasure of this call?" Whenever she speaks with that nasally voice, my hand can't help but clench.

"Serena. I would like to talk to you about the school. Can you swing by Dad's today?"

She smacks her lips. "I suppose so. I'll drop what I'm doing and entertain your idea."

I pinch the bridge of my nose and try not to tell her where to go. "Thank you. I'll call and order from that favorite restaurant you like."

"Wonderful. I'll bring Roan he would love to visit."

"Perfect," I fake cheer.

"Bye, Odette." The line goes dead, and I throw my phone on the couch.

"Don't you ever make me do that again? I swear I could've punched her through the phone. And before you ask, yes, Roan is coming." I sink on the couch, resting my head on the back. I'm not mentally prepared for this.

Maddox walks into the living room, dragging a chair. "Wilde should be here in half an hour. Should we get things set up?"

"Yeah, where do we want him?" Ashton grabs the chair and looks at Atticus.

"Well, not in here. Hide him someplace they won't see or hear him."

I point toward Dad's office. "That would be the ticket. It would be ideal since I want to discuss the school with Serena."

Ashton moves to Dad's office. "This I can't wait for. I need some more excitement in my life." He chuckles.

Yeah, it's official. I'm rethinking this plan. Ashton and Maddox are both gonna enjoy it. Atticus will just be an asshole, and I will have to wait forever to get my answers. It shouldn't matter if I get answers, but justice needs to be served. They can't get away with it.

Watching Wilde tie Augustus to the chair makes my stomach flip. Having him in this house doesn't sit right. In a way, I feel like I'm betraying Dad by having his murderers come into his home. He better not come back and haunt me. I'm doing him a favor by doing all of this.

"You hear that, Dad." I look around the office, making sure he knows.

"He knows, Jinx. Don't worry," Wilde says, tying the last knot and backing away. "And this house doesn't give me the vibe of being haunted. You're good."

I narrow my eyes at him. "Where the hell did you come from?"

"Parkview. Don't ask. That place is a dump compared to this place."

"I hope this works. Where the fuck is she?" Atticus cuts in.

"Who knows, she's your mother." I brush past him. Knowing her, she'll be fashionably late. I should've given her a time. This is bullshit waiting around for her. I move to the living room and peek out the window. Her ears must've been ringing because I see her white Cadi roll into the driveway, and my stomach drops. "Fuck."

I watch her and Roan step out of the car, laughing at each other. Roan takes her hand kissing it; they look like a couple in love, not a couple that can plan anything vicious. Her voice rings out, and my hand clenches. I need to remind myself to play nice until this is over.

They walk in like they own the place, and when Roan sees me, he grins. "Ahh, Odette, what a lovely surprise."

I roll my eyes, what a douche. "I bet it is. Seeing how you knew I was here."

He goes to say something, but Serena puts her hand on his shoulder. "That's enough, you two. I swear you are like children. Shall we start with lunch?"

I raise a finger. "Actually, can we start with business? I would like to get that out of the way."

Roan nods. "That's a good idea. I would like to know the sudden change of mind."

"Okay. I set everything up in Dad's office." I extend my hand toward the office. Roan leads, followed by Serena. The closer we get, the more I can hear Dad's heartbeat. This is finally over. Roan places his hand on the office doorknob, and fear claws at my throat. God, this can go so wrong.

They both stagger inside when they see the twins standing before Augustus. I shut the door behind me, locking it and sealing all of us in. Maddox and Wilde stand to the side, watching, waiting. The air grows thick with anticipation. Atticus moves to the side, and Serena inhales sharply.

"What is this?" She presses her hand to her chest.

"I think you know, Mother. The gig is up. We know everything, he squealed like a fucking pig. We know you killed Prescott."

She rushes forward, smacking Augustus across the face. "How could you? We had a deal!" she screams. "After all this, and you ruined it."

Augustus laughs low. "No, you fool. You ruined it. They didn't know who killed Prescott." He stares at her. "You squealed like a pig, you fucking idiot. After all these years, you still can't keep that mouth shut."

Roan turns to leave, but Maddox is on him. "I don't think so, asshole." He kicks the back of his knees, dropping Roan to the floor. Roan tries to fight him off, but Maddox pulls his arms behind his back, lifting them upward.

"I won't stand any of this. You have nothing on me."

"They do. I told them about you stalking Odette. If I go down, you go down," Augustus taunts.

Roan snaps his head to the side. "How could you? We had a plan; stick to the plan, you asshole."

"What plan?" Serena demands, looking between them.

Augustus sighs loudly. "To pin everything on you, but you had to remove the old man's heart for some sick and twisted desire. Couldn't let the poor man be whole even after he was dead."

My brain can't keep up with any of this. Serena killed Dad? "Why? Why did you do it?"

"Simple child, for the money," Roan says.

"What money. Serena wouldn't get any, and she knew this," Maddox spoke through clenched teeth.

Serena's laughter rang out. "You expect me to believe that. He owned a school, for Christ's sake. He's holding back on me."

"Serena, you were there with the lawyer. There is nothing for you. You killed him for nothing." Pain grips my throat; the thought of him sitting in his office talking to her, not knowing what she was planning, kills me. She was his wife; even if she didn't act like it, how could she do that to him? All for money that was never there.

"And you asshole, why did you start stalking Jinx?" Ashton asks the other question everyone's been dying to know.

Roan looks at me with a bored expression. "For intel mostly, but she became rather fascinating when the twins showed up. I couldn't help but make myself known. Do you think I was only stalking you since they showed up? Think again; it's been years, you just never knew it. I know everything about you. But it became fucking hot when Atticus took you for the first time, I had to tease you."

Atticus storms over, landing a punch to Roan's face. "You fucking prick." Roan falls onto his side, groaning. "I should kill you."

"That doesn't sound like a bad plan. Maybe not fully, but enough that he'll need a wheelchair for the rest of his miserable life," Ashton adds, slamming his foot into his ribs. Roan rolls over, grabbing his side.

"Stop, you'll hurt him." Serena rushes over, wrapping herself over Roan.

"Yeah, that's kinda the point. Eye for an eye, Mom." Ashton grabs Serena and hauls her off, handing her to Wilde. She screams when Atticus lands another punch to his face, and an ear-splitting crack fills the air. I don't think I can watch this. I back up, reaching for the door;

blood pools on the floor under Roan's broken face, and it's flashbacks to Dad's office. I can feel my throat closing up, and the room spins. I turn, facing the door, flinging it open.

The cool air of the hallway is welcoming, but I need more. I slowly make my way along the walls towards the kitchen until I reach the patio doors. Feeling overwhelmed, I drop to my knees and let the tears flow as I rest my head on the window.

After all this, this is how it ends. No, I want my fucking justice. I want them all to rot in jail. Dad doesn't deserve anything less. His legacy doesn't need to be tainted like this. I need to be the daughter that he raised and demand more. But I won't be able to do it alone if the guys keep taking rounds out of Roan. They'll end up in trouble too. I brace myself and stand. This all ends today.

I head back to the office, and Serena's screams can be heard from the hall. I brace myself for what I'll see in the office again, but it needs to be done. I stare at the floor in the doorway and take a deep inhale. Lifting my head, I try not to look around.

"That's enough!" I yell.

Atticus halts his move; his foot frozen in the air. Wilde still has Serena in his arms, her hair a mess from fighting; when I look at Augustus, he has a bloody nose.

"I can't let you guys keep doing this. I need to call the cops."

"Jinx, are you out of your mind?" Atticus stands, his knuckles bloody and on display.

"No, Atticus, I'm serious. They need to pay for their actions, and I know who can help."

Maddox crosses his arms, trying to hide his hands. "Who, Jinx?"

"Barnaby. He's always been on my team in every board meeting, and I trust him. He can help, I promise."

"Jinx, we just beat the shit out of Roan that doesn't look good." Ashton points to Roan's body. I stare at Ashton, knowing I won't be able to look down.

"I know, but can you please trust me?"

"Okay. Tie Mother up, and we'll clean up. Call him first before the cops."

I turn to leave when Ashton says, "Jinx, I'm sorry."

"I know." I leave them to clean up, grab my phone from the couch, and dial Barnaby's number.

Praying he'll help.

Twenty-Nine

Jinx

Barnaby has been in the office for an hour, and he didn't hesitate when I called him to explain some of what happened. I'm thankful for that; I couldn't explain everything over the phone. I curl up further in the chair, pulling the blanket to my chin—a chill races down my arms, thinking about that office.

Every time I close my eyes, I see that pool of blood under Roan's head, and I'm scared to see what he looks like now. I still haven't found out where Dad's heart lies. But I believe he's at peace inside, and that's all that truly counts.

"Baby?"

I glance over and watch Maddox walk into the living room in a clean shirt that Burnaby must've brought.

"Do you need anything?" He kneels in front of me, rubbing my leg.

I reach out for his hand, and he gently intertwines our fingers. Watching his hazel eyes soften fills me with warmth. "Maddox, after this is all over with, can we leave?"

"Yeah, of course."

I shake my head. "No. Leave this entire place. I don't want to be here."

"Running from your problems won't solve anything, Jinx. They have a habit of following."

I drop my chin on my knee. "Fuck. I guess you're right. Should I ask how it's going in there?"

"Barnaby is actually cool for an old guy. He's got contacts out of the ass, so we have nothing to worry about."

"What about Serena? What's gonna happen to her?"

He laughs. "Oh, her ass is going to jail. Burnaby called his cop buddy; he'll be here shortly. Augustus and Roan will both be joining her, too. You have nothing to worry about there. It's over."

"But is it? I'll never be the same. Nothing will be the same. She killed him for nothing. I'll never be able to forgive her."

"And you don't have to. No one says you do. You take things at your own pace and do things your way."

"Maddox? Can we have a word with Jinx," Atticus interrupts.

Maddox leans up, giving me a gentle kiss. "Take it easy on them; they feel guilty." He pushes away and pats Ashton and Atticus on the shoulder as he walks past them.

Both guys glance over at me, matching pale blue eyes and tousled blond hair, each with that charming cupid's bow when they smile. It's always startling to see how much they resemble each other. They even move the same. It's so freaky. They approach me, Ashton sitting on the arm and Atticus standing before me.

"Jinx." Atticus clears his throat. "I can't imagine how you can look at us without feeling hate towards us."

"Why would you say that?" I was speechless; where would this come from?

"It's because Mom killed your Dad. How could you not look at us and not see her? We have her fucking eyes, for Christ's sake, and hair color."

I turn to Ashton. "Ashton, that's not the same thing. Just because you look like her doesn't mean anything; she isn't you, or you, Atticus. I would never hold that against you." I glance over to Atticus.

"But you could. What if you get married? Who's gonna walk you down the aisle? When you have a baby, they won't have a granddad. All because Mother ruined that for you." Atticus drops to his knees, wrapping his arms around mine. "I'll never be able to forgive her."

"Atticus, look at me." I tip his chin upward. "You don't have to forgive her, but thinking about the future won't do you any good. Focus on the now, here with me, Maddox, and Ashton."

"I can try, but if, for some reason, you start to resent me, walk away. Promise me, Jinx."

"I promise."

"Burnaby wants to talk to you. Did you want me to get him?" Ashton asks.

"Yeah, but I'll meet him in the kitchen. I need a drink."

He chuckles. "Alright. Are you sure you're okay?"

"I think so. Maybe with time, things will be better."

He leans over, kissing my forehead. "You tell me if things get bad."

"I promise."

He pushes himself forward and heads for the office. Atticus pats my knee and stands. "Let's get that drink."

I'm halfway through my drink when Barnaby, Ash, Maddox, and Wilde walk into the kitchen. Barnaby grins at me, grabs a glass, and pours himself some whiskey.

"What a day, Odette. What a day." He raises his glass and slams it back.

"You're telling me." I finish the rest of mine and wait for whatever Barnaby wants to say.

"My cop friend will be here shortly, and he'll take Serena into custody. He'll need a statement, of course, and we'll use Augustus and Roan to help the charges stick. I have lots of faith here, and you shouldn't worry. You did the right thing by calling."

"You're sure she'll go to jail?"

"One hundred percent. We have no worries anymore."

As my shoulders relax and the weight of the stress begins to lift, I am filled with relief. Those words I've been eagerly waiting to hear have been spoken. I can't wait to see her in court and hear the words *guilty* as she's carried away.

"Did she ever say where Dad's heart is?" I look around, hoping they know.

They all shake their heads. I guess I was never meant to know.

Wilde decided to stay in Grovedale; I guess the town grew on him, and I'm glad he found a place to call home, but it's almost sad to see him go, even if he wasn't around for that long. He's always welcome back anytime.

I close the laptop when Spence ends his stream, place it on the coffee table, and stretch my arms above my head. It's been a busy few days after Serna was arrested, in and out of the police station, lawyer visits, and then the news broke around the school. I couldn't walk anywhere without whispers and fingers being pointed. The guys suggested I take a break and book a hotel room in the city to get away for a while.

I just didn't know they all would be joining me.

I look over at the bed and see them all lying there watching TV. And what a sight it is. Maddox chilling with his hands behind his head, showing off his six-pack while his pajama pants hang low on his hips. Atticus chilling in the center, leaning against the headboard adorned with tattoos all over his body. My eyes move to Ashton, and I chuckle. The only one wearing a shirt and pants. His eyes snap over to mine, and he runs his hand down his body and winks.

"You can unwrap me later."

I choke on my laugh. "Oh, God."

"Get over here, Little Grim."

I move over to the bed and crawl on top of Atticus to lie across all of them, never to leave anyone out. If I knew this would be my life, I wouldn't have fought it for so long. Well, I might still fight Atticus because getting on his nerves is half the fun. Each one has brought something new to my life with new adventures, and I can't wait to see what the future holds. I'll never go a day without feeling love, hope, and torment because they like to bring that out. But I wouldn't change it.

NEVERMORE

About the Author

Hello, loves! I'm a Canadian romance writer who's all about the steamy and dark stuff. Horror books, movies, and music? Yes, please! I have a little true crime obsession, but I'll just call it research and pretend it's normal.
If you crave love stories that push the limits of lust, trust, and desire, you've come to the right place.

Follow me for exclusive sneak peeks, giveaways, and behind-the-scenes glimpses into my writing process. And if you want to keep up with my latest releases or connect on social media.

Let's dive into the shadows together, darlings.

ALSO BY

A HITMAN'S DUET
MYLES

CARTER

RUSSO MAFIA SERIES
UNBROKEN

UNBEARABLE

UNDENIABLE

STRANGERS OF EASTWOOD
STRANGERS OF THE NIGHT

STRANGERS OF THE TOWN

STRANGERS OF THE CROWD

RAVENWOOD ACADEMY
ATTICUS

ASHTON

MADDOX

STANDALONE
CHRISTMAS UNWRAPPED

PAINFULLY MERRY

SWEET DREAMS